THE WOMAN'S RIGHT

THE WOMAN'S RIGHT

A story of my Maine grandmother
1848–1927

Franklin F. Gould, Jr.

iUniverse, Inc.
New York Lincoln Shanghai

The Woman's Right
A story of my Maine grandmother 1848–1927

iUniverse books may be ordered through booksellers or by contacting:

iUniverse
2021 Pine Lake Road, Suite 100
Lincoln, NE 68512
www.iuniverse.com
1-800-Authors (1-800-288-4677)

ISBN: 0-595-34286-8

Printed in the United States of America

To both my wives Marion W. and Marian S.,

No man was ever luckier

Foreword

I hardly knew my grandmother. Throughout my early years I was probably aware that she was a remarkable woman but I had little interest in researching her life. During my teens whenever I did ask about her, I sensed reluctance on the part of those who remembered her to say more than that she was still a righteous Christian in spite of her divorce. But in recent years as we have heard more about liberated women, her contribution to our present-day culture has become apparent to me. How many women have modeled their lives after hers? How many have said:

"She did it. So can I."

I don't know the answer. But as one woman who took her destiny into her own hands, she deserves whatever fame I can give her.

The narrative that follows, as some readers have probably already noticed, is subtitled "A" story and not "The" story of my grandmother. I make no claim that as the chronicle unfolds the emotions described or the neighbors' reactions are as they happened. They are as I imagine them. I do insist that every one of the major characters existed. The former slave boy, Jericho, who attached himself to my grandfather at the end of the Civil War, is not fiction, but any part he played in the matrimonial plans of Tom and Lizzie is my concoction. I even gave him his name and explained how he got it. Or in another case, Dad used to tell me of a comical and profane friend of his father known throughout the community as Horace "By God you mister" Jordan, and I could think of no one more fitting to make commander of the Lisbon Falls

G.A.R. Post. All family members are in the right order and each accomplished the work I say he or she did as far as I have been able to determine.

The same goes for the letters, diary excerpts, newspaper articles, etc. Many of these I have copies of. Some I do not. It seemed ridiculous not to devise an answer when I had the question in the handwriting of the questioner. Then there are other times when my narrative skills prompted me to make up both questions and answers. All quotations from Grammy's book, however, are authentic. Beyond that, I have no intention of revealing which items are sourced and which are not. I'd prefer they all be considered accurate renditions of the truth.

Most of the dialect needs no explanation. When a State-of-Mainer says he "sawr it", you know he has had some education, otherwise he would have said he "seen it". Although an "r" in Maine-talk may appear between vowels even when it isn't "theyah" (as with "sawr it"), it is always left off words like better (bettah) and sugar (sugah). I have avoided this last problem (and several others) by allowing most of my ancestors to speak ordinary English.

For the typical reader two Maine words in the first chapter need explanation, since they continually reappear throughout the novel. They are "ayuh" and "dhow". "Ayuh" means "yes", possibly derived from "aye, yes", expressing something a little more positive than a simple affirmative. "Dhow" is an emphatic negative. To avoid bewildering my listeners when I am talking to summer folks and other non-Mainers, I seldom use either word except when under stress.

Once while I was lecturing to my New-York-bred students in SUNY Oneonta, I digressed briefly with an illustrative anecdote. A student interrupted to inquire: "Will this be on the exam?" I looked at him in disgust. Why would anyone seriously expect an exam question on a throw-away side-bar? I reverted to my childhood response to stupidity.

"Dhow" I replied.

"What the Hell does that mean?" the class asked in unison.

"Yellow eye" is the name of a popular baking bean. "Up attic" and "down cellar" are other legitimate Maine-isms,. as is "cultch" (used to identify almost anything that's not wanted or is in the way), and "dite" (a small amount) but even an Iowan should be able to figure out what they mean without footnoting. I usually make that assumption when I permit my relatives to talk as my relatives always did.

BOOK ONE

CHAPTER 1

"There she be, Tom—comin' out the church door—the gal in the green bonnet. I brung you out here on to the street so's you'd get a good sight at her."

"Jumpin' Jehoshaphat! Frank, would you take a look at her?"

"Soon as I set eyes on her, I said to myself right off, I said, Tom Gould's got to see this lady."

"You sawr 'er yesterday, you said?"

"Ayuh. When I was down to Miss Emma Foster's millinery shop. She's Miss Emma's young sister."

"You was in Emma Foster's place? What in tarnation was you doin' in there? Buyin' lace for your stovepipe?"

"I was with Lil when she picked up that new hat she's rigged out in this mornin'. Here comes Lil, now, out o' the church. All fancied up. She's stoppin' to talk to Miss Emma and her sister. In a minute she'll bring 'em over here, so's we can meet 'em."

"Jehoshaphat," Tom repeated, reaching up to smooth down his hair, straighten his cap, and run his fingers across the bristle of his short beard.

It was after midday on Sunday, June 24th, 1866. The two young men were standing in front of the Methodist Church on the main street of the rural community of Lisbon, Maine. At the top of the church steps the congregation was filing before the youthful pastor who stood near the entrance. Frank's sweetheart, Lillian Wallace, smiling prettily, shook the preacher's hand and exchanged a few words with him, then glanced in Frank's direction and nodded. She slipped her hand under the arm of the eighteen-year-old girl in a green bonnet who stood beside her.

Only a few weeks before B. Franklin Farrar had been mustered out of the Union Army to return home to the girl he loved. He was a small man, hardly tall enough to peer on tip toes over the five-foot hedge that grew between the roadway and the church lawn, but in his high hat and trim frock coat, he was by far the jauntier of the two young men.

It had been a year since Sgt. Thomas J. Gould was honorably discharged from Company J of the 16th Maine Infantry, but he still was wearing the pants of his blue uniform. Only a couple of inches taller than Frank, he found himself rising on his toes as he studied the women descending the steps.

"You gotta quit cussin' like Johnny Reb, Tom," Frank whispered, "If you're plannin' to be courtin' one of the Foster gals. Emma's a real lady and I figger her sister's one too."

"She might be wuth it," said Tom. "Wha' didja say her name was?"

"I recollect Emma called her Lizzie, but I ain't real certain. Wha' didja think of the sermon. He's a candidate to preach here."

"Pretty fair for a beginner."

"Only pretty fair? You gotta put more vinegar on your beans than that, Tom, if you're figgerin' on impressin' the Foster gals. The preacher's Caleb Foster, their brother."

"You never told me she was the preacher's sister."

"That's right."

"Must be quite some family to have a parson in it. Quite some family."

"That's why Lil an' me hauled you over here this mornin'. When we heard their brother Caleb was preachin', we figgered the Foster sisters would be here with bells on. We figgered even a Free-Will Baptist like you could go at least once to the wrong meetin' house, if it meant you was to find your future bride."

"Lookee here, Frank, five years ago you talked me into enlistin' in one war. Don't you and Lil go gettin' me involved in a second one."

"Hush," said Frank, grasping his friend's elbow. "Here they come…." He removed his hat and bowed as the women appeared around the hedge. "Well, well, Ladies, that was certainly a fine sermon your brother gave this mornin'. Very fine."

"We're especially proud of Caleb," Emma said.

"Franklin," Lil said, "You know Miss Emma Foster and her sister Elizabeth?"

"I sure do. I met Miss Elizabeth yesterday."

"Ladies," Lil continued, "This is Mr. Thomas Gould, a local farmer. He and Franklin served together all through the War. Since Frank got back," she teased, "I declare he spends more time with Tom than he does with me."

"Don't say such foolishness, Lil," Frank responded. "Tom and me've got a pile to talk over." He looked to Tom for agreement and then turned back to the women. "I hain't seen Tom since I transferred outa J Company in '63. Tom sawr a good deal more real fightin' than I ever did."

"Oh, yes," Emma said, "Everybody in Lisbon knows about Mr. Gould. I pointed out 'our war hero' to Elizabeth this morning when you entered the church."

"I'm pleased to make your acquaintance, Miss Foster," Tom said. He stood awkwardly with his cap in his hand, embarrassed by the tribute and uncomfortable with the obvious conspiracy to push him into the arms of this dainty child who stood gazing raptly into his face with two of the bluest eyes he had ever encountered.

"I have so much admiration for you brave men who fought in our tragic war," Elizabeth said. "Thank the good Lord it has finally come to an end."

"Tom and me was just remarkin'," said Frank, changing the subject abruptly, "That perhaps you ladies would like to accompany us on a walk down to the Ten Mile Falls. It ain't far an' it's easy walkin'. It's particularly handsome this time o' year. On account o' the drought, the Androscoggin River ain't so high as it might be, but there's still plenty o' water in it."

"That would be most pleasant, Mr. Farrar," said Emma. "But we must be back by two-thirty. Caleb is having dinner with us and he must have time to rest before evening services."

"That'll give us plenty of time," said Frank.

"Then by all means. I'm sure Lizzie will enjoy the view."

"I was glad when Tom suggested it," said Frank, elaborately giving his friend credit for his own notion.

"I think it's a grand idea," said Elizabeth. "I'd love to see more of your friendly community."

"I'm full o' good suggestions," said Tom, winking at his fellow conspirator.

CHAPTER 2

The stroll through the village to the Androscoggin River was most congenial. Miss Emma, her parasol twirling slowly in the bright sunshine, joined Frank and Lil as they walked some distance ahead of Tom and Elizabeth. The pair at first continued in silence.

"Emma tells me you served the entire duration of the War," Elizabeth finally remarked when she realized that Tom was having difficulty finding something to say. He nodded. After a moment he replied:

"Somewhat, I guess. They mustered us in, Frank and me, in '62." He paused briefly, before adding: "In August." After another pause, longer, as if he were trying to decide how to phrase his sentence: "On the same day. Both of us." He nodded thoughtfully again, before he explained: "I guess I'd a probably gone sooner, but I had to wait till after my twenty-first birthday. My father claimed he needed me on the farm, but just as soon as I was old enough, I signed up anyways."

"What a courageous thing to do."

"My brother stayed to home. Father thought he wa'n't old enough to farm, but Levi did all right. The farm's still there."

"Levi's your brother?"

"Ayuh."

"How old was he?"

"I don't know. Fifteen or so, I guess," He hesitated, obviously becoming aware that this line of conversation was leading nowhere. Then he blurted: "But you don't want to hear any more about my worries. I'd rather find out about you and what you're doin'. You're visitin' your sister?"

"That's right."

"Be you in Lisbon long?"

"No, I'm leaving tomorrow. I've been here almost a week. I came up because I knew Caleb was going to preach today."

"I liked what he said. A considerable."

"The family's very proud of Caleb."

"You plannin' to come back to Lisbon soon."

"I do hope so, but it depends. Emma says they're looking for a teacher for one of the Lisbon schools. She's going to ask Mr. Leighton if I may apply for the position. He's the Supervisor of Schools and Emma knows his wife pretty well. If he says yes, I'll come back for a meeting with the Committee. I'm inspired by the possibility."

"A school teacher, eh? Now, that takes genuine spirit. There's some real roughnecks in the Lisbon schools. Pea Eyes from Canady."

"They're just boys. I know all about boys. I have three brothers. Boys don't frighten me. Even Pea Eyes. I know some very nice people from Prince Edward Island."

"I think you're brave."

"I think that's a very nice compliment coming from a soldier who has faced the dangers you have faced."

At the lower end of Main Street a zigzag path, with wooden steps constructed at the steeper slopes, led down the rocky incline past the cotton mill to a wide ledge thrusting out into the stream. Tom offered his right arm and Elizabeth placed her left hand on it and, to facilitate her descent, raised the hem of her skirt with her right. As the footing became more precipitous, Tom felt her fingers tightening. At that moment he vowed to himself he would speak to Leighton the very next day and make sure the teaching position was offered.

From the ledge the view upriver was majestic, with streams of water plunging like iridescent plumes between great granite boulders. Daisies and orange hawkweed dazzled the wide grassland above the mill. Across the river maple and beech overhung the river bank, their lower trunks concealed in a tangle of alders and blackberry bushes.

"Oh, Mr. Gould," Elizabeth exclaimed. "I'm so grateful you suggested this walk. This is, indeed, such a beautiful place. Just listen to the tumultuous roar of the waters, and—yet—it is so peaceful, as if all the evil discords of the world have been drowned out. Do you come here often?"

"Once in awhile. I was down here earlier this week, lookin' at that stand o' hardwood over there."

"It's so inspirational."

"Old Whitcomb owns it. I heared he wanted to sell so I come down here to look it over."

"My gracious, don't tell me you are planning to buy those lovely woods."

"Dhow, I figgered gittin' the cordwood across the river would be more trouble than it was worth."

"My, Mr. Gould, you certainly sound like a practical man."

"I plan to be."

Miss Emma had found a seat nearby where, during thousands of past springs, flood waters had worn a shelf in the granite. She called to her sister.

"Couldn't you stay here forever, Lizzie? It's so serene. Come here and sit for a moment under my parasol. I'm so pleased that Mr. Gould suggested we join them on a stroll down here. Just look at the glorious field up there beyond the mill, all aflame with color. Tell me, Mr. Gould. Do you know what those flame-colored flowers are?"

"They're hawkweed."

"What a dreadful name for such a lovely blossom," Miss Elizabeth commented.

"Deserves it," said Tom. "You let it git into your hayfield and you might as well say goodbye to your hayfield. If that field was mine, I'd be right out there now turnin' it under, Sunday or no Sunday. See here. Here's one o' them hawk-weeds agrowin' right here in this crevice. They'll grow anywheres. See these flat leaves at the bottom. They spread out all around the stalk and kill the grass. That leaves bare ground for the seeds to take root in. Another couple o' days after the blow is gone, the air here'll be full o' hawkweed seeds, floatin 'round lookin' to cause trouble like so many Seceshers' observation balloons, worse than dandelions. Daisies ain't much better."

"Why, Mr. Gould," Emma said, startled by his sudden volubility. "You sound as if hawkweed were your enemy."

"Ask your brother, Miss Emma. The good Lord tells us in His parable: the enemy comes in the night and sows tares among the good seed…"

"Whoa, Tom," Frank interrupted with a pleasant laugh. "Don't get carried away and start argufyin' with the preacher. We all know the enemy ain't gut a chance when you git started. Did he tell you, Miss Lizzie, about the time durin' the Battle of Spotsylvania when General Whipple rode up on his horse and shouted, "Stop shootin', Thomas. You've killed enough?'"

"Where'd you hear that one, Frank?" Tom asked. "That's one o' my brother Levi's fabrications. I thought he took all them yarns with him when he lit out for the Maritimes."

"Go on with it, Tom. You told me that one yourself."

"Didn't you tell me, Frank," Lil asked, "That it was Spotsylvania where Tom was wounded?"

"That's right, wasn't it, Tom?"

"'Twa'n't much of a wound," Tom insisted. "Lots o' times I skun my knee a lot worse when I was a young un tearin' 'round the barnyard."

"Why, Tom, you didn't tell me you were wounded," Miss Elizabeth said with a shudder but with evident admiration. Tom noticed that she referred to him by his first name.

CHAPTER 3

When the Civil War ended Moses Foster (father of Emma, Lizzie and their brother Caleb as well as four other offspring) was a cobbler in a small farming community in inland Maine. Against this backdrop of rock-strewn hills and fields and surrounded by his lasts, awls, and the other tools of his trade, he might have appeared to a casual observer to be the typical bumpkin.

But his small enterprise was located in the town of Gray, the halfway point on the thirty-five-mile Post Road running north from the bustling Portland waterfront to the twin cities of Lewiston and Auburn, where during the War the power from a forty-seven-foot falls on the Androscoggin River had produced an explosion of industry and population.

Next door to Moses' shop was the Gray Road Tavern, where hungry travelers made regular stops and legislators, heading to or from the state capital in Augusta, frequently lodged for the night. It didn't take (as the disparaging byword current at the time expressed it) "a pair of Mormon spectacles" to see that events of consequence could not occur anywhere in the nation—and probably the world—without evoking a spirited discussion among the businessmen of Gray. Moses saw himself as being in the thick of things.

He was alert to opportunity. When Ezra Blake from Lisbon, a town twenty miles to the east, stopped by to have his boots tapped, Moses wanted to know why.

"What's the matter with my friend Hiram in Lisbon?" he asked. "If you took your boots to him, you wouldn't have to make the long trip over here."

"Hiram ain't well. Been laid up most o' the spring. These days a person's got to go out o' Lisbon for 'most everything. Even dressmakin', the wife claims she's gut to go all the way to Lewiston to find a seamstress."

"What happened to Mabel Townshend? Thought she had a good business."
"Hain't you heared? Mabel gut through two weeks ago."
"Mabel's dead? I'm sorry to hear it."

The next morning Moses rented a horse and buggy at the livery stable and drove to Lisbon, bringing with him his nineteen-year-old daughter Emma. Through business acquaintances in Lisbon he located a respectable widow, Mrs. Joshua Rounds, who would provide his daughter room and board. He rented a small office space on Main Street where a work shop could be set up. Then he placed a notice in the weekly Lisbon *Enterprise:*

Miss Emma Foster, trained in Dressmaking and Millinery, on Monday next will be opening an Establishment two doors up from the Town House where she will be available to ladies of fastidious taste to assist them in choosing, designing and assembling ATTIRE and BONNETS of the LATEST CUT and FASHION. Reasonable rates—available upon request.

Emma was delighted. At that time her older sister, Sarah Jane, was doing ordinary housework in Portland, although she had ambitions as a writer. Emma pictured dressmaking as being much more refined. During Emma's childhood, Mrs. Freeman, an elderly neighbor in Gray, had been teaching her the rudiments of fancy sewing. Together they had pored over the Ladies Book and other fashion journals, extracting whatever concepts they could adapt to the materials they had available. Now, through her father's association with Portland warehouses she obtained an assortment of exotic feathers and gimp as well as ample bolts of fabric to begin her business. Within a year she had developed a substantial clientele.

When she learned in a letter from her father that her brother Caleb had been invited as a candidate to preach at the Lisbon Methodist Church, she asked her landlady if she might invite her younger sister Lizzie to visit so she could hear their brother's sermon.

Mrs. Rounds, a sweet, diffident lady in her sixties, had found in Emma the daughter she had never had. As soon as Emma had moved in, she suggested she be called Auntie Rounds. There was little that Emma asked for that was not granted. The old woman agreed that she would love to have Elizabeth come, and also insisted that Caleb should be invited to Sunday dinner after the morning services.

❦   ❦   ❦

Although the two young women returned promptly from the stroll to the Falls, Caleb was already awaiting them in Mrs. Rounds' parlor. The landlady was distraught. Dinner was cooking in the kitchen but to leave a parson unattended was unthinkable. She was standing in the doorway to the dining room, moving her generous weight nervously from one foot to the other, when Emma and Lizzie appeared on the front porch.

"Where on earth have you two been?" Mrs. Rounds demanded as they entered. Emma laughed.

"Are we late, Auntie Rounds?" she asked. "I'm sorry. We took a little after-meeting tramp. I guess you could say we've been finding a husband for Lizzie."

"What a wicked thing for you to say," Lizzie protested while coyly smiling. "I only remarked he would make some young woman a proper husband."

"My goodness," said Mrs. Rounds, forgetting for the moment the urgency of the kitchen, "What on earth have you two been up to?"

"Indeed," Caleb agreed. "I would say that pronouncement demands an explanation. It seems to me that a little bird has been whispering in my ear that Lizzie has been seeing a good piece of a certain JDR."

"That wretch," said Lizzie. "Don't mention him to me."

"The last time I heard," Caleb continued to tease, "The sun rose and set around JDR."

"I found him out. He's truly a wretch."

"Then who is this latest paragon?"

"There is no paragon," Lizzie insisted tartly. "Emma's just teasing because a local young gentleman assisted me as I climbed down a steep embankment to view the falls. I hardly remember his name."

"Maybe not but he certainly seemed entranced with something and all the time I thought it was Lizzie," Emma said.

"A local young gentleman?" asked Mrs. Rounds, stepping back into the center of the room. "Now, who on earth do you suppose that could be?"

"You tell them, Lizzie," Emma said.

"As I recall, Lil Wallace introduced him as Mr. Tom Gould."

"Mr. Gould! Mr. Tom Gould?" Mrs. Rounds exclaimed, joyously clapping her hands. "Why, his sister-in-law is probably my best friend. Emma, you know Aphia Gould."

"His sister-in-law?" asked Emma, obviously startled by this information. "Aphia's husband is Tom's brother? I thought he was at least his uncle. He must be fifty years older than Tom."

"My gracious sakes, no. Jake's not that old. What on earth are you thinking of? To say a thing like that. Why, he's younger than I am. Him and Tom, you know, are actually half brothers. Jake's mother—Mary—she was such a dear, sweet lady—she passed on years ago and then old Jacob—that's Jake's father—married Rebecca Hinckley. At the time there was some bad talk, as I remember. It was only months after poor Mary departed this life and Rebecca was less than half his age…"

Caleb raised his hand to stop her but he found a mere gesture was insufficient to part the Red Sea of Mrs. Rounds' volubility. She surged on:

"Rebecca was at least three or four years younger than Jacob's own children, but then—I guess—it turned out to be a good marriage. How on earth would anybody know? They had two other children besides Tom. There was Mary and Levi, but Mary died. Still a baby, only three years old. Would you believe it, he named her after his first wife.…"

"We aren't hankering after the whole Gould family history quite yet, Mrs. Rounds," Caleb interrupted. "Tell us about this Tom Gould, Lizzie. Was he one of the young men standing on the roadway after services this morning?"

"Yes, he was," Lizzie nodded.

"The one in the tall hat?"

"No, the one with the cap."

"He looked presentable," said Caleb.

"Oh, he is," Mrs. Rounds volunteered. "He owns a big farm up on the Ridge. Far as I know his father left it to him lock, stock and barrel, just so long as he provides a home for his mother and Eunice—Eunice is Jake's sister, Tom's half-…."

"What's that I smell?" asked Caleb, lifting his nose and sniffing the air. "Something in the kitchen?"

"Oh, gracious," said Mrs. Rounds. "You'll have to excuse me."

"There," said Caleb as Mrs. Rounds dashed from the room to see to the dinner. "Now we can discuss Lizzie's *in amorato* without interruption. Tell me, did you have much of a conversation with this Mr. Gould?"

"They must have found a great deal to talk about," said Emma, when Lizzie hesitated. "They walked side by side all the way down to the river and back. But excuse me, too. I must go help Auntie."

"Was Mr. Gould in the War?" asked Caleb when they were alone.

"He told me he volunteered in '62," Lizzie said. "I suspect he was quite a hero, but he wouldn't talk much about himself. When I asked him about the War, he abruptly changed the subject. He must have had many painful, dangerous experiences. His friend, Mr. Farrar, intimated that he makes jokes about his ordeals rather than discuss them openly. Mr. Farrar did say Tom was wounded in battle but Tom immediately dismissed his injury as if it were trivial. He is certainly a very valiant man."

"Oh, ho. Tom, is it?"

"I can see no harm in referring to a friend by his first name, even if he is of short acquaintance."

"If you didn't discuss the War, what did you talk about?"

"We discussed his farm. He is clearly very proud to be a farmer and he knows so much about nature. He asked me about my coming to Lisbon to teach school."

"Then he didn't speak to you of his 'most disastrous chances, of moving accidents by flood and field, of hair-breadth scapes in the imminent deadly breach, of being taken by the insolent foe and sold to slavery.'"

"Of course he didn't. Don't you quote the Bible at me, Caleb."

"That's not the Bible, little Lizzie. It's William Shakespeare. That was what Othello, the Moor, said about wooing Desdemona. Othello said, 'She loved me for the dangers I had pass'd and I loved her that she did pity them'. I think your swain missed an opportunity when he spoke of farming instead of fighting."

"You and your quotations, Caleb," Lizzie retorted. "Do you memorize everything you read?"

"You've heard Father say that being able to produce an apt quotation's the mark of a true scholar. Besides, I read Othello only last week and I thought his speech about courting Desdemona quite grand. This is the first opportunity I've had to quote it. I can give you more, if you would like."

"You've given quite enough. I think you're rude to make a mockery of me. I just took a stroll in the company of Emma and her friends, and that's all that happened. I found Mr. Gould to be a remarkable gentleman, and if I should ever return to Lisbon, I would be pleased to have him for a friend. I would appreciate your not making more of it."

"Lizzie, you know I'm just being affectionate. As your older brother I do want you and your sisters, all of you, to be happy. So many of the young men who have returned from the War were hardened by their experiences. Don't become involved with anyone just because you pity them for the 'dangers they had passed.'"

As he reached out and took Lizzie's hand, Emma called from the dining room to say that dinner was ready.

CHAPTER 4

During the stroll to the Falls, Frank Farrar had left his little horse and two-seated gig in the carriage house behind the church. He offered to drive Tom back to his farm.

"Tain't much out o' the way and I'm drivin' that direction anyways to take Lil home."

"Just drop me off at the four corners."

Hanging on with both hands and sitting sidewise on the outside of the narrow seat, Tom was quiet and thoughtful. Even when Lil remarked on the refinement of the Foster sisters, he had little to say.

"They seemed sensible," was his comment.

When they reached the place where the Gould Road crossed Sabattus Pike, he jumped out, nodded a quick "thank you" to his friends and started jogging down the half-mile stretch to his farmhouse. His thoughts were awhirl with plans of getting married and starting a family, ideas that never before had occupied his mind for more than a passing moment.

"Sarjent Tom," a voice called. Tom paused. A black boy about ten years old, barefoot and clothed in a cut-down Union uniform, was sitting nearby on the stone wall under the shade of a giant oak.

"Hello there, Jericho. What in tarnation are you doin' settin' there? Did you git the tie-up cleared out, as I told you?" The boy climbed down and joined Tom.

"Yassuh, Sarjent Tom. An' I harness up Fan an' druv de women folks to choich, jes' lak you say."

"That don't tell me why you were settin' here on this wall."

"Jes' come up t' walk down the hill with y'all," the boy said.

"You got somethin' on your mind?" The boy nodded, but said nothing as they continued toward the farm. But after a while the words poured out.

"Miz Eunice, she sorrowful upset you weren't drivin' her and yo' momma t' choich this mornin'. She don't take to me. She say, what'll folks say when dey see dem Goul' women bein' druv to choich by a colored slave. Ah don't like dat kinda talk. Ah jes' clear out an' come up here t' bide fer you."

"You shouldn't let Eunice aggravate you, Jericho. She says a lot of things she don't mean. You just inform her that you're no slave."

"I 'form her dat. She say, Don't you sass me. She say, Jericho don't git no pay. She say dat make Jericho a slave."

"She can go plum to blazes. You ain't a slave, Jericho. You came North with me of your own free will and accord—because you didn't have any place else to go. You can leave any blamed time you please. In the meantime, you've got a roof over your head, a place to sleep and plenty t' eat."

"Ah know dat. Ah's mighty grateful to the good Lord ah found you when ever'body ah knowed was skeedaddlin' off like skeret water bugs. Warn't nobody left on th' plantation but colored folks an' ol' Miz Hayden an' her young uns, an' they all lit out witout me. An' mos' o' de Yankee sojers paid me no mind. Ah was mighty hongry when you come by. But dat don't mean Miz Eunice got cause t' go callin' me a slave."

"Jericho, I'm sorry," Tom said, putting his hand on the young fellow's shoulder. "I'll speak to Eunice and tell her not to say things like that to you…That corner we fixed up for you in the loft's a lot better than sleepin' on the ground, ain't it?"

"Reckon 'tis," said Jericho. They walked in silence for some distance, the grasshoppers in the hot dust springing in every direction to avoid being stepped on. Finally, Jericho spoke again:

"Massa Jake tell me, he say I c'n git a payin' job in the woolen mill."

"You mean my brother? When did you talk to Jake?"

"Yesterd'y."

"What right has that son of a second-hand seacook got puttin' ideas like that in your head? He didn't pick you up out of a Virginny cowshed an' bring you back to Maine. Of course, Jericho, you could git work in the mill, but you know you're hell-fired better off right where you be. I'll speak to Eunice and put a stop to this slave talk."

"Yassah, Sarjent Tom," Jericho said, as they reached the back door of the house and the black boy headed for his quarters in the barn.

❦   ❦   ❦

"Mother," Tom called, as he walked into the kitchen.

"I'm in here, dear," his mother replied as she peeped from the pantry. "You weren't to services this morning."

"Frank Farrar asked me to go to the Methodist Church with him. He had somebody he wanted me to meet."

"Who was that, dear?"

Before he could answer, Eunice, who was sitting in the corner of the kitchen, spoke.

"Thomas Gould, don't you ever do that to your mother and me again. I was so ashamed, ridin' in that carriage like a couple of Southern slave owners with that pickaninny of yours driving. What do you suppose folks in Lisbon are going to say?"

"Don't go gittin' all haired up, Eunice. Jericho likes to manage the mare, makes him feel like a reg'lar stage driver. He was real tickled this mornin' when I asked him to drive the two o' you to church. When Frank came by and asked me to go to meetin' with him; first, I didn't know what to do. Then I thought, Jericho can do it. He's been drivin' Fan all over the place, handles her clever as a jockey. So I asked him, and he was tickled pink. You shouldn't be telling him he's a slave. It only makes him discouraged. The poor fellow's pretty lonesome, as it is."

"Well, that makes no difference to me, so long as I don't have to ride with him. All I'm thinking about is what people will say."

"Who in blue blazes gives a hellity-whoop what people say?"

"Tom, dear," his mother said, wiping her hands on her apron as she entered the kitchen. "You've got to stop using such rough talk. You're not in the Army any longer, you know. Tell me, who was it that Frank wanted you to meet? Some comrade-in-arms?"

"No, Mother, it was the girl I'm goin' to marry."

"Marry? Why, Tom Gould!"

"Yes, Mother, the girl I'm going to marry."

"What are you saying?"

"You know Emma Foster? The milliner."

"You planning to marry Emma Foster?"

"No, no. Not Emma. But you know who Emma is?"

"Not, really. I've heard Aphia mention her. She lives with Bess Rounds, doesn't she?"

"I understand," Eunice said, "that she's a very resourceful young woman." The word *resourceful* sounded almost obscene in Eunice's mouth. Tom ignored his half-sister.

"Well, this mornin' Lil Wallace introduced me to Emma's sister. She's goin' to teach here in Lisbon. We walked together down to the Falls and I just said to myself, right off—This is the girl I'm goin' to marry."

"Did she agree to marry you?" his mother asked.

"I never asked her. I just thought about it. It was when I was coming home, I decided."

"Don't you think it might be up to her to decide?" Eunice asked.

"She'll say yes, all right. I ain't worried about that."

His mother laughed and turned to Eunice.

"When Tom makes up his mind, everybody had better take heed. He's just like his father. What's her name, Tom?"

"Name? By thunder, I don't know. Now, what was it Miss Emma called her? She called her something, but I'll be derned if I can remember what it was."

CHAPTER 5

Tom spent the morning of the following day mowing hay in his lower meadow. From soon after daylight until noon he swung his scythe like a metronome, cutting even swaths across the field, stopping only at the brookside to scoop up in his hand a mouthful of water or occasionally to take his whetstone from his hip pocket and stroke it across the blade. After noon he hung the scythe and snath over the limb of an oak tree and gave Jericho instructions for tedding the hay for drying. As he had pledged to himself the day before, he harnessed Fan to the wagon and drove over the Ridge to the Leighton place on the River Road. Mrs. Leighton told him that Jed was in the cornfield.

"Good to see you up and around, Tom. What's on your mind?" Jed asked, straightening up and leaning on his hoe.

"Just passin' by, Jed. Stopped to say hello."

"That don't sound like Tom Gould to me. Never knowed a Gould not to have something on their mind. Can't think of a blamed thing I've got to trade, Tom. Maybe in a couple o' days I'll be havin' some pigs. The sow was groanin' this mornin' so's it looks like she'll litter anytime."

"Got more hogs now than I know what to do with," Tom said, as he stooped to pull out a handful of witch grass at the base of a cornstalk. "Corn's doin' nicely."

"Dry, though," said Jed. "Got to keep hoein' all the time."

"Gettin' some rain later this afternoon."

"Think so?"

"Aye yes. That's what Eunice says and it sure feels as if. They tell me the School Committee's lookin' for a teacher."

"Not any more, we ain't. The Missus found me a top-notch candidate. We're callin' her in for an interview next week."

"Local woman?"

"Not exactly. You know Emma Foster, who runs the hat shop down in the village."

"Ayuh."

"It's her sister, Elizabeth. Hannah Elizabeth Foster, but she's called by her middle name. The Missus says Emma calls her Lizzie. She's from over Grayway. Why you askin'?"

"Just inquirin'. I've heard good things about Miss Foster. She'd be a good 'un for ya…. It's good to see things goin' all right for you, Jed. Guess I'd better be gittin' back to my hay before the rain gits here. Jus' thought I'd stop by."

"Good to see you, Tom. Give my regards to your mother and Eunice."

Jed again leaned over his hoe and Tom drove back home.

🍁   🍁   🍁

Jericho was shaking out the last swath of hay when he looked up to see black thunderheads boiling up from behind the Ridge.

"Gwine t' rain, Ah reckon," he said aloud. "Sarjint's hay gwine t' git wet but that don' make no nevermind t' me. Ahse done."

As he threw his pitchfork over his shoulder and started to climb the slope toward the barn, there was a glimmer of lightning along the horizon and a few moments later the rumble of distant thunder. He looked toward the top of the hill, hoping to see Tom returning before the rain came.

Far in the distance at the crossroad, he spotted Fan, the Morgan mare that Tom was so proud of, moving at a fast trot, her chestnut coat and black mane flecked with white foam. She swung around the bend onto the Gould Road and started down the hill, the wagon behind her bouncing dangerously on the exposed ledges. Heavy, black clouds swept swiftly across the zenith, covering the sun. Now, Jericho could make out the oncoming wagon only when the lightning flashed.

"Tain't lak de Sarjint to drive dat-away," he said. "'Stoo late now t' save his hay crop from de wet."

Sensing something was amiss, he dropped his pitchfork and ran toward the house, arriving just as Fan slowed and turned into the yard. She came to a stop near the barn door. Tom was sprawled on the wagon seat, his legs extended, his head thrown back and his face ashen, his left hand clutching his right side. He tried to rise.

"Jericho. Quick!" he called feebly. He wavered a moment and then collapsed. Jericho jumped into the wagon beside him. He placed his arm over Tom's shoulder and pulled him gently down until he was stretched along the seat.

"'S awright, Sarjint," he murmured. "'S awright. Jes' y'ol' camp fever agin. Easy, now, Sarjint. Don' y'all try to move, now. Ah'll fetch yo momma."

As he ran toward the house, lightning and a stunning explosion of thunder brought forth a drenching deluge. Ignoring the pelting rain, Jericho reached the doorway and yelled.

"Miz Goul'! Miz Goul'! Sarjint Tom been took agin."

He beat on the door and shouted louder. Tom's mother peered through the kitchen window.

"What's that Jericho want now, Rebecca?" Eunice asked from where she was sitting. "The lightning scare him?"

"It's Tom," Tom's mother screamed. "Something's wrong with Tom."

She rushed out into the downpour, with Eunice not far behind.

"It's the Rebel ague again," Eunice cried. "I'd guess he didn't take his quinine."

"Poor Tom," said his mother. "Will he never recover? After the last siege, I hoped he was better."

Soon the three of them were partly carrying, partly leading the shaking, shivering veteran through the driving rain into the house. They stretched him out on the couch in the corner of the kitchen.

"Here, Rebecca, here's a blanket," Eunice cried. "Wrap him in this blanket. Jericho, help Rebecca wrap Tom in the blanket. Look at him shiver. Can't we get some of those wet clothes off him?"

"He's hot as a spider," Rebecca said, holding her hand to Tom's forehead. "Can you reach the quinine, Eunice? That's right, thank you. Now, measure out the calomel…Not that much. No more than a pinch. Here, let me give it to him and you go find the castor oil."

"Sarjint Tom, please, Sarjint Tom," Jericho pleaded.

For nearly two hours Tom lay groaning on the couch.

His mother, still in her wet clothes, soothed his forehead with a damp cloth soaked over and over in the cool water Jericho had brought up from the deep well in the cellar. Eunice was hovering nearby with blankets and dry garments. Tom's severe shaking and shivering passed and did not return, but his fever dropped only gradually. Little by little the pain in his side abated. When he finally opened his eyes, Jericho was again standing nearby, watching him anxiously.

"Did you rub Fan down, Jericho?" Tom asked.

"Yessah, Sarjint Tom. Jes' the way yo showed me. She's in the barn, all dry."

"You're a good boy," said Tom, and he closed his eyes. In a few moments he spoke again, this time without looking.

"Mother, her name's Hannah Elizabeth."

"Whose name's Hannah Elizabeth, dear?"

"The woman I'm goin' to marry, Mother. They call her Lizzie."

CHAPTER 6

❀

Throughout that watchful night after his malarial attack, Tom aroused intermittently to ask his mother or Eunice, as they took turns by his bedside, whether Jericho had shaken out the wet hay. Each time they assured him that it was not yet daylight; that the hay would be taken care of as soon as possible.

Early in the morning Eunice went to the barn for Jericho, but he failed to answer when she shouted his name.

"Now, where do you suppose that boy's gone?" she called through the kitchen door to Rebecca.

"Sh," Tom's mother whispered back, "I think Tom's fallen asleep. The pain must have gone. His fever seems down. Why don't you see if Jake can help?"

Eunice strode down the road to her brother's farm. Passing the lower meadow she saw little Jericho already at work, the drops of water on the grass he had turned over glistening in the morning sun like snow flakes.

"Young man," she called. "Are you sure you know what you're doing?"

"Yes'm, Miss Eunice. Jes' de way de Sarjint tol' me."

Later that day, after everything had dried out, Jake and his son Niah came up the hill, harnessed Fan to the hay rig and brought the hay crop to the barn. They told Jericho to climb to the mow in the loft and tread it down.

🍁   🍁   🍁

Gray, Maine
July 16, 1886

Thomas J. Gould, Esq.
Lisbon, Maine,

My dear Mr. Gould—

I have just returned to Gray after another visit to your pleasant community where I was offered a position as teacher in the Webster School. I had a gracious interview with the Lisbon School Committee on last Tuesday evening and Mr. Leighton, the chairman, notified me the following day that they had voted to offer me employment. He told me then that you had generously spoken on my behalf.

I shall begin teaching in September, but I have not yet decided whether to come to Lisbon where I can reside with my sister Emma or to go to the town of Poland where I also have been offered a position and is some nearer to Gray and my family. My older sister, Sarah Jane, has recently gone to Harper's Ferry in West Virginia to teach the freedmen. She has suggested I join her, but I don't believe I am ready to go so far from home. My father urges Poland and I shall probably obey him.

I had expected to be able to thank you for your kindness at church services on Sunday, but learned instead that you have been laid up for several days. Emma tells me that you have suffered a recurrence of the terrible swamp miasma with which so many of our brave soldiers have been afflicted.

Remember that for those who love Him, "the Lord will…take away all sickness" (Deuteronomy 7:15). I will pray for your rapid recovery.

With warm regards,
H. Elizabeth Foster

Tom was sitting in the sunshine near Eunice's flower garden when his half-brother, returning from his weekly visit to the Post Office in the village, brought Elizabeth's letter. Tom was still pale, but he told Jake the pain was gone, his strength was returning and he was steady on his feet again. In the last few hours he had made several trips to the barn for small chores without ill effect. In another day he expected to be back to normal.

"I'll bring up the *Enterprise* for you to read when we're through with it," Jake said, as he headed down the hill toward his home.

Tom read the letter from Elizabeth several times before showing it to his mother.

"I told you she'd have me," he said.

"Aren't you taking a lot for granted? Remember, you haven't asked her yet."

"I figure she didn't have to write. She must have wanted to keep in touch with me."

His mother shook her head, and in mock dismay was uttering a rueful "Tom" when her face suddenly brightened.

"So that's where you went Monday. You went over to see Jed Leighton, didn't you? To ask him to hire this Miss Foster of yours. Tom, I do declare, you're just like your father. When you set your mind on something you don't let any grass grow under your feet."

"It worked for him. If he hadn't stormed the battlements to reach you, I wouldn't be here today."

"For heaven's sake, Tom. Don't let Eunice hear you talk that way about her father."

"What about Eunice? She's got to get used to the idea of having a woman around the house who's got as much spunk as she has."

His mother smiled and again shook her head.

"Eunice probably wouldn't appreciate hearing you use a vulgar word like 'spunk' to describe her, either," she added as she handed Elizabeth's letter back to him.

❧　　　❧　　　❧

Lisbon, Maine
July 20, 1886

My dear Lizzie,

I hope you dont mind me using your first name, but after your welcome letter I feel like we are pretty good frends. I am feeling much better. The doctor says I have probably had my last bout with the fever. He says you sort of grow out of it after a time. I hope he noes what hes talking about. I am back working and not too soon. I had cut most of the best hay all ready. But what was still in the field was almost gone by and the weeds were choking out my garden. It was some bad luck to be striken down right at this time of year. I hope you chuse to come to Lisbon, because I am looking forward to seeing you again. Even if you go to Poland, I hope you will likely be coming to visit your sister once in a wile here in Lisbon and maybe I can see you then. Whatever you do, don't go to Harper's Ferry. Even if you don't come back to Lisbon, I hope you will write to me again because I like to get your letters. If you do go to Poland like your father says whatever you do dont get mixed up with those Shaker folks that I heer have a colony there. I heer there mighty good people hardworking God fearing honest and all that, but they dont let men and women mingle and I dont think that is such a good idea. I heer they take in orphans, but they teach them theirselves, so likely you wouldent be seeing much of them anyways. I hope you dont mind this little piece of advice. If you get a chance write me what you decide. Perhaps your sister could tell Mrs Rounds to send me word through Aphia when you are visiting again in Lisbon and we could go to church together. Aphia is my sisterinlaw she noes Mrs Rounds.

Yr True Friend
Tom Gould

❧   ❧   ❧

August 10, 1886

Dear Tom—

My father has convinced me to take the teaching position in Poland. I shall be living with a fine family named Merrill right on the road to Gray so I shall see my family on many week-ends. Although it is nearly a two mile tramp to the school house, two of the Merrill children will be in my school, so in inclement weather I expect to ride snug and dry with Mr. Merrill, who says he always drives his children to school on unpleasant days. The Poland schools always close during heavy snow storms, they tell me.

I expect to be in Lisbon to visit Emma—for the last time before school starts—on the weekend of the 26th, and will be pleased to attend church with you. Perhaps you would prefer to go to the Free-will Baptist Church, which I understand is your usual choice. If so, the Baptist Church it will be.

You may rest assured that while I am in Poland I will not fall under the influence of the Shakers. I already know several members of that faith for they frequently have done business with my father. Although I have a great deal of respect for them personally, I also find, as you do, little to commend in their separation of the genders.

I hope this letter finds you in good health. After the first of September my address will be c/o Mr. Wordsworth Merrill, Poland, Maine.

> With warm regards,
> H. Elizabeth Foster

CHAPTER 7

"Where can I get me a coat, Frank?" Tom asked his friend when the latter stopped by the farm on his way into town.

"A coat, didja say? Or a goat?"

"A frock coat, like the one you was wearin' Sunday."

"Where you goin' where you'll be needin' a frock coat?"

"Why in tarnation should I be goin' anywheres, Frank? I'm already here."

"Thought maybe you was goin' to go to Indianapolis."

"Indian Apple where?"

"Didn't you read about it? The first encampment."

"What encampment?"

"You know. The G.A.R. We was talkin' about it the other day. The Grand Army of the Republic. Some fellars out West in Indiana are organizin' it. Didn't you read about the encampment in this week's *Enterprise?*"

"Hain't seen this week's paper. Aphia ain't through with it."

"The G.A.R.'s havin' their first national encampment in Indianapolis. On November Twentieth, I think it said. When you said you needed a coat, I guessed maybe you was plannin' to go."

"You goin'?"

"Shucks, no, Tom. Wished I was."

"Wouldn't it be great? You know, Frank, if anybody'd ever told me I was goin' to miss the Army, I'd a said he was plumb off in his head. But somehow—it's hard to say just why—but somehow you don't feel whole back here on the farm. Like there's some part o' you missin'."

"I know what you mean. I couldn't wait to get back to Lil and yet, there still was an empty feelin' when we was mustered out." Both men stood quietly for a moment, staring off toward the horizon. Then Frank said: "But if you ain't goin' to the encampment, Tom, wha'd'you need a frock coat for?"

"Just figured I'd need one to wear to church. Maybe I'll even get me a beaver, while I'm about it."

"It'll be Jubilee day, Tom Gould, when you spend your filthy lucre on a hat. Specially, so long as you've got an old one."

"You can go plumb to Tophet, Frank. Maybe, I've got a good reason why I want to look respectable. Maybe, I'll just go ask somebody who don't fire all this bunk at me."

"O.K., Tom, you win. I bought my coat in Lewiston. Old Mabel Townshend used to do tailorin' here in Lisbon but she warn't much good at it. Anyways, she's passed away. Emma Foster only works on women's things. An' mostly bonnets. The tailor I went to's on Lisbon Street right after you get into the city. He's a foreigner. Eyetalian, I guess. Does a good job, though, and don't cost you an arm and a leg. You'll like him soon as you figure out what he's talkin' about."

Just before he went to bed on Saturday, the 25th of August, Tom told his mother that if she and Eunice wanted him to drive them to church the next day, they would have to be ready early. He was planning to pick up Miss Foster as soon as he dropped them off.

"Don't we get a chance to meet her?" Eunice asked.

"Not till after meetin'"

"She'll be real proud to be seen with you in your new coat and hat, Tom," his mother said.

"Now you tell me, Lizzie, that Tom Gould's escorting you to church this morning," Emma said. "What about that Cyrus fellow you were telling me about? The one over at Sabbath Day Lake? I declare, I simply can't keep track of all your swains."

"You don't have to keep track of them, my dear sister, so long as I do. I wrote Mr. Gould some time ago, and told him I would go to church with him this morning. 'That Cyrus fellow', as you call him, is a nephew of Mrs. Merrill, the lady I am staying with in Poland. He has been most diligent in courting me, but I have made no commitment, nor do I intend to."

"Well," said Emma, still teasing her younger sister, "If you don't mind, I'll just walk on ahead by myself, rather than wait to chaperon you and your friend."

She started to open the front door. Lizzie tossed her head and replied with feigned superiority.

"Mr. Gould and I will be going to the Baptist Church, you know, so I doubt very much that he will be offering a ride to a Methodist like you."

"We'll soon find out. He's pulling up in front of the house right now. If anyone should ask me, and I'm sure nobody will, I'd say he's not driving a very fancy carriage…But just look at his new outfit—a mulberry coat. He certainly looks neat and tidy…for Tom Gould. Do you suppose he actually bought a new coat and hat just to take you to church?"

Lizzie dashed to the window.

"My gracious," she cried. "Doesn't he look handsome? He must have bought them with me in mind. Oh, Emma, don't you think we make a remarkable couple?"

"Why, Lizzie. How you talk."

Tom pulled Fan to a stop and threw the reins over the dashboard. He reached the front door just as Emma came out.

"Mr. Gould's here, Lizzie," she called back into the parlor. "I'll see you after church."

"Come in, Tom," Lizzie said. "I'll be ready in a moment."

Tom stood awkwardly in the doorway, holding his new hat in both hands, while Lizzie, gazing up into the mirror over the fireplace mantel, positioned her bonnet with elaborate precision, tucking certain wisps of hair under the brim and pulling others out to form a filigree about her forehead.

"That's a real pretty hat," Tom said.

"Why, thank you, Tom," she replied. "My sister loaned it to me from her shop. I think it's lovely.

"She ought to let you keep it. It matches your eyes."

"Do you really think so? How nice of you to notice. That's a new coat, isn't it, Tom?" she asked over her shoulder. "It's certainly handsome."

"I figured I couldn't wear my old Army duds if I was taking an extry-ordinary woman to church, so I found me a tailor in Lewiston to make me a new coat."

"Oh, what a nice thing for you to say, Tom. Well, I guess I'm ready." She moved quickly toward Tom, retrieving a dainty aqua parasol from an umbrella stand as they passed through the door.

"You look special to me," Tom said. He helped her into his buggy. "I guess if I'd turned Fan around before I pulled up in front of the house, it would of been easier," he commented as he picked up the reins.

"This will be just fine," she said.

"Fan's gentle. She's easy to handle. Even on this narrar street she'll turn real easy."

"She's young, isn't she?"

"Aye yes, bought her one time durin' the War when I was home on furlough. Soon as I seen her, I knew I had to have her. Spent most o' my back pay on her, but she's wuth it. She'll be foalin' for the first time next spring."

"Do you have other horses?"

"Not right now. Just oxen. Maybe, I'll keep Fan's colt. I'll see in the spring."

"That sounds like a good plan."

"I'll see. But Miss Lizzie, you don't want to hear about my plans."

"Oh, yes, Tom. It gives me so much pleasure to talk to a man who so obviously is proud and happy with what he is doing. So many men I know don't have plans. To hear them talk, one would believe that life is an empty vessel and they have no idea how to fill it. You are so full of enthusiasm about your farm."

"I've got plans, all right, Miss Lizzie. Would you like to see my farm?"

"Very much."

"I been hopin' you'd say you wanted to see it. Mother'll be at church this mornin'. You'll meet her after service and I'll suggest she invite you to come visit us. Maybe for dinner. You goin' to be stayin' in Lisbon all week?"

"My brother Avery is coming to get me on Wednesday."

"Is that your preacher brother?"

"No, Avery's my younger brother. He still lives at home with my parents."

"I'll tell Mother then to invite you tomorrow and I can come pick you up. How does that strike you?"

"Strike me? Oh, Tom. What a bold expression? Of course, that will be fine."

"I been thinkin'" and he reached over and took her hand.

"Yes, Tom."

"If you like the farm, I'm plannin' to ask you to be my wife."

After a moment, he glanced hesitantly toward her, but she was gazing straight ahead. From where he sat he was uncertain whether she was pleased or pained by his bold announcement. Although he couldn't be sure it was a gauge of her reaction, he observed that she had stopped twirling her parasol. He accepted it as a good sign.

CHAPTER 8

Early Monday morning, as soon as his chores were finished, Tom killed and dressed a plump cockerel, stopped by the garden to dig a hill of new potatoes, and brought the produce to the kitchen. He directed Eunice to find some eating corn in the patch beyond the sty. As he left to fetch Lizzie, he told his mother that dinner should be served at noon. The two women were now busy carrying out his orders.

"You're right, Eunice," his mother was saying as she added dry alder wood to the stove to "het" up the oven. "Tom's never been around women his own age much. You don't meet girls in the Army. Do you guess he'll ever get bold enough to ask Miss Foster to marry him? It's one thing for him to tell his mother he's going to, but quite another to do it." She stooped and drew a green-apple pie from the oven. She set it on the back of the stove and replaced it with a pan of buttermilk biscuits. "Poor Tom," she remarked as she straightened, "He's got his heart set on this girl but he's quite bashful, you know."

"Bashful!" Eunice hooted. "Poor Tom, indeed. Sometimes, Rebecca, I worry about you." She opened the door to the cellar and lifting the cover from one of the earthenware crocks that stood in the passageway, forked several pickles into a bowl. As she re-entered the kitchen she continued: "Tom's about as bashful as 'Nezzar, Papa's old bull. You've said yourself: When he puts his mind to something, there's no stopping him. Wouldn't surprise me a bit, but he'll have a contract with this Miss Foster all signed, sealed and delivered by the time he gets back here this morning."

"Eunice, sometimes I think you're wicked."

"Well, I may be wicked but I'll tell you one thing," Eunice said as she placed the bowl of pickles on the table and began slicing them. "If he takes his Miss

Foster up to see the maple grove, one or the other of us had better plan to go along with them."

"I would expect Miss Foster to ask one of us to go with them. I hear she's very proper."

"They must be coming!" Eunice cried, glancing out the window. "Jericho's racing toward the road with that new dog of his yapping at his heels. I guess he's seen Fan turning the corner."

❦   ❦   ❦

Tom swung the buggy on to Gould Road and started down the hill. Lizzie was captivated by the valley panorama.

"Is that your house—the first one—with the hipped roof?" she asked as Tom nodded proudly. "My gracious, it's huge. And look at the barns. And the garden. Is that your pasture beyond the stonewall with the sheep in it? It's beautiful, Tom. I never imagined it would be so beautiful."

"I come this way apurpose," Tom explained, "so's you could see the view. Comin' up the hill's a dite shorter, but 'tain't near so pretty."

"Thank you so much for bringing me this way. Drive slowly, so I can enjoy its beauty. It's hard to believe you tend this great spread all by yourself."

Tom reined in Fan and squared his shoulders.

"Jake—he's my half-brother—and his boy help me once in a while. They live down the road. We sort of work together. And my sister Eunice—you met her at church yesterday—she helps out in the gardens. We say the flowers are all hers. Durin' hayin', sometimes, and plantin' I have to bring in a man, and that time when I was sick, but most of the time I'm alone."

"This was your family's farm?"

"Aye yes, my father built the buildin's himself. T'warn't nothin' but woods here in '86 when he got his land grant from Massachusetts. He cleared all these fields and built the house and the barns. Even killed his own bricks for the chimley. Of course, after my half-brothers came along, they helped. Hain't changed much since I was born."

"From Massachusetts, you said?"

"Aye yes, that was before Maine was a state, back when we was just a province of Massachusetts."

"That was a long time ago. Your father must have been an old man."

"Only a few weeks short of ninety-five when he died in '62."

"My goodness."

"Look," Tom cried as he turned the carriage into his dooryard. "Here comes Jericho with his new dog."

"Jericho?"

"Aye yes. Brung him back with me from the War." He reined Fan to a halt. "There you are, Jericho, you hold Fan while Miss Foster gets out. That's a good boy. Then, you can lead Fan into the stable. Don't unhitch her, but you can give her some water. We'll be goin' back into the village later on."

"What do you mean," Lizzie asked, "When you say you brought him back from the War?"

"Yes, indeed. Right after Petersburg. While we was foragin', I found him hidin' in the rubble of a barn the Union cannon had blasted to smithereens. Hadn't eaten, I guess, for a couple days. He hitched himself on to me like a leech and come on home with me. Ain't that right, Jericho?"

"Yessuh, Sargent Tom, jes' lak a leech." Jericho threw his head back and laughed.

But this conversation was cut short when Tom's mother called from the doorway.

"Welcome, Miss Foster."

Tom led Lizzie into the house, while Jericho clutched the collie pup by the scruff of its neck to prevent its jumping up on the newcomers. "Down, Stonewall," he ordered. When the couple disappeared into the house, Jericho led Fan to the barn.

As Eunice had predicted, after the meal Tom invited Lizzie to walk to the maple grove so she could inspect the farm. She accepted readily. But Lizzie did not suggest, as Rebecca had expected, that one or both of the older women accompany them.

After they left Eunice remonstrated but Rebecca insisted:

"Eunice, you stay out of this."

The couple strolled along the stone wall that marked the edge of the pasture, up a rutted roadway that was established over three-quarters of a century before to haul timber and firewood down from the forest and over which each spring daily trips were made to tend the fires at the sugar house. Tom pointed out the beehives near the apple trees below the barn.

"Tell me," Lizzie said somewhat sternly, "About Jericho. Just who is he, anyway?"

"I told you. He followed me home from the War."

"But what about his family?"

"As far as I know, he hain't got any family."

"Are you making any effort to locate the boy's mother?"

"Don't you worry about Jericho. He's all right. He was kind o' lonesome, but I got him a dog and he's all right now."

"What about his learning? Is he going to school?"

"He can write his name. I taught him how."

"His name? Is Jericho really his name? What's his last name?"

"I don't think he knows what his last name is. He didn't even know his first name till I gave him one."

"You named him Jericho?"

"Well, the men did. When he sort o' joined the company, the men wanted to know where he hailed from. I told them he must o' come from Jericho, 'cause his walls had all fell flat. The men picked up on that and started to call him Jericho. I guess he likes his name all right, 'cause…"

"You're saying the boy's name came from a joke you made? Why, Tom Gould, you sound as if it makes no difference. I suppose you also named his dog Stonewall."

"I thought it was a pretty good name for a dog. Don't you?"

"It's shocking. A boy or a dog. Just give him a funny name."

Lizzie pulled away from Tom and stood with her hands on her hips.

"What kind of religious instruction is the boy getting?" she demanded.

"Now, Lizzie."

"Don't you 'Now Lizzie' me. That boy should be going to school."

"He's gettin' good trainin'. You saw yourself how he handled Fan. Hain't many lads that age can handle a horse."

"The next thing you're going to tell me is that he sleeps in the barn." Her eyes were blazing.

"Why not? I fixed up a good place for him."

"Oh, Tom. Don't you see. He deserves so much more than this. There's a Methodist mission in Portland. Jennie—that's Sarah Jane, my elder sister—she works for them. She's down in West Virginia today teaching darkies just like Jericho to read and write. She's telling them about the Gospel and the words of our Savior. Negroes like Jericho have to learn, Tom. It's our duty to broaden their brows."

Tom bristled. He was unaccustomed to having a woman tell him his duty.

"Jericho gets three meals a day," he said. "And a good place to sleep, and I learn him all he needs to know. He don't need missionaries to tell him what to learn."

"No, no, Tom. We must take him at once to the Mission in Portland. They will know how to teach him to use his freedom."

Tom straddled the lane, his eyes narrowing. "Jericho stays where he is," he said. "He's happy. He don't want to go any place else."

For a moment Lizzie was speechless. She could not believe that Tom had finished the discussion. She searched his face for a clue to the argument that would convince him of the rightness of her position, but found only finality.

"Come, now, Lizzie," he said offering his arm. "I'll show you the rest of the farm."

She drew her lips together tightly, and scarcely moving her jaw uttered between her teeth:

"I have seen all of your farm I desire to see. You may take me back to my sister's residence."

"Now, wait a minute."

"No, Tom. Your treatment of this child is an abomination." Tom was bewildered. His anger was mounting.

"You come here to see the farm, and dammit you're going to see it," he growled, grasping her arm.

She pulled herself loose and walked briskly toward the house.

"There is never a need for profanity," she said without looking back. "I am sure that if you won't do it, your mother will see to it that I am returned to my sister's."

"Now, wait a minute." He started toward her but she quickened her pace.

"You have your choice, Tom Gould. Either you harness up your horse, or I shall walk back to the village."

She was moving rapidly, her skirt switching up small wisps of dust from the edges of the pathway. Tom stood still. For a moment a shadow crossed his countenance as if he were about to tell her she could damn well go ahead and walk. But as she approached the backdoor, he decided to avoid a confrontation with the women inside.

"Hold on," he growled, "till I get Fan."

CHAPTER 9

"August 31, 1866

"Dear Diary,

"Before Father left today to go back to Gray after dropping me off at the Merrill homestead, he gave me this beautifully bound diary-book with a hasp and a lock. I believe he acquired it from the salesman from the T. B. Mosher Publishing Co. who stops at the tavern. Father speaks of him often. It looks very expensive, but I am certain Father did not pay full price. He mentioned that I should keep a record of my teaching experiences in Poland, as well as my thoughts and a catalogue of the books I shall be reading. I shall start keeping my journal Monday, September 3, after the first day of school. He said it was only a suggestion but he will surely be asking me whether I am following his advice. It is my purpose to keep you diligently, dear Diary."

Lizzie was true to her word. Every evening before going to bed she meticulously copied into her diary an account of the day's activities, first writing it out on a separate sheet to make positive that the grammar and punctuation were correct and the words were spelled properly. Her first mention of Tom Gould was in the entry for September 16:

"…At services this morning the Rev. Crossman described Joshua and Caleb entering the promised land and my mind turned immediately to little Jericho. Do you suppose Tom Gould ever did anything about that poor boy? I do hope so, because I would like to believe that he is still contending for the cause for which he so nobly risked his life. I wonder if he ever regrets—or even thinks about—having announced to me that he planned to ask me to marry him…"

She mentioned him again on the twenty-first:

"One of my students mentioned today that his mother's given name is Eunice. The only other Eunice I know is Tom Gould's elderly half-sister. Emma has told me Eunice is older than Tom's mother. How strange…"

On the thirtieth:

"…I have been introduced to several young men in the community by Mrs. Merrill. Wilbur Rowe is the elder brother of Dicky, one of my students. At church this morning he offered to walk me home and was very gracious and polite, but he does not seem to have the character that I am looking for in a man. I wonder if Mr. Gould ever did anything about Jericho's education…"

There were still other references on later dates.

Meanwhile, Tom could not get Lizzie out of his thoughts. When Frank Farrar married his Lillian, Tom was filled with desire. Perhaps if he approached Lizzie as if nothing had happened, she would forget the things she said about him and Jericho. After several hesitating starts, he wrote her a letter.

Lisbon, Maine
Nov. 26th 1866

My Dear Lizzie,

A lot has happend since you begun teaching in Poland. My friend Frank Farrar got married a while back to Lil Wallace. You remember them. They was with us last June when we walked down to see Ten Mile Falls after church. I guess you probbly no about them allready because your sister Emma was at the wedding, too. Likely she even made Lil's dress. I looked around hoping you would be there. I here that after you decided not to come to Lisbon to teach they hired a man for the job but he didnt work out too good,—I guess he drinks. Theres been a good deal of talk here in Lisbon about starting a post of the Grand Army of the Republic. You know, for the Veterans. If they do, I guess I will join up. Do you think thats a good idea??? How are things going for you in Poland. I hope alright. I hope you don't mind me riting to you, but I thought you might like to catch up on things in Lisbon. I been thinking about you a good deal, espeshally since Frank and Lil got married, so I thot Id rite and ask you to rite and tell me the news. How are things going for you in Poland. Do you like teaching??? I think about you all the time.

Things are going good here on the farm. Busy with fall things—otherwise this letter would be longer. My mother sends her regards. Yr true friend, Tom Gould

❦   ❦   ❦

**c/o Mr. Wordsworth Merrill
Poland, Maine
December 4, 1866**

My dearest Emma,

You will never guess what happened this week. I received a letter from Tom Gould. Nice as pie. Never once mentioned the Negro child, Jericho. He made no effort to explain his behavior nor to apologize. He wrote just as if nothing had ever happened between us, as if we were still the closest of friends. What do you make of that?

I shall never forget that afternoon he brought me back to your place. I kept expecting him to apologize, but he sat up stiff as a fence post and never looked one way or the other. He is certainly a stubborn man. Of course, I was not speaking to him. I was so glad to see you on Mrs. Rounds' porch when we drove up, because that avoided any need of my saying goodbye to him. He stopped only long enough for me to get out and away he went. It was really quite amusing, looking back on it. As you suggested, I wrote a brief note to Mrs. Gould thanking her for inviting me, without explaining the circumstances of my sudden departure. Do you suppose he ever told her?

Of course, I shall not reply to his letter. When I wrote Jennie what I had done, she agreed that it was the right thing. And so did Father. I shall just let Tom Gould stew.

I am happy teaching in Poland. The small children like little Hiram Ricker, can be such a joy. However, several of the older boys are giving me trouble. I cannot write some of the terrible things they say and two of them seem to have no interest in learning whatsoever. One keeps threatening to leave school and sometimes I think it would be best for everyone if he did. At times, I hope his parents will encourage him to do so. Oh, dear Emma, you are so fortunate to be making hats out of ribbons and laces and not trying to make adults out of children.

You remember my telling you about Cyrus. He still diligently courts me, which I find flattering, but I have not given him any encouragement. He is so shallow, with no dedicated interest like farm or a business. There is another young man with whom I have been walking, but I shall not tell you his name, because then you will tease me as you did about Cyrus. Besides, I have heard that his father paid for a substitute to keep him out of the draft, which I would consider unacceptable in a young man. Although that may not be true, I do know it is fact that he was never in the War. I tell you these "bits of news" so you can see I am not allowing Tom Gould's outrageous behavior to interfere with my social life.

I have started keeping a diary as Father suggested. I find it most difficult to write my innermost thoughts, even when I know that what I say is only for my eyes. However, I find it is good practice in composition. In addition to my activities, I am keeping a record of all my expenditures. I am sure it will be helpful in years to come to have this history to refer back to.

I hope you will be able to come home for Christmas, for I am so looking forward to seeing you. Jennie will be there. She has returned from West Virginia and is now at the Mission headquarters in Portland.

Your loving sister,
Elizabeth

The sisters wrote regularly to each other. It was three months later that Emma wrote this letter:

c/o Mrs. Joshua Rounds
Lisbon, Maine
Thurs., Mar. 14, 1867

Dear Lizzie,

I usually do my letter-writing in the evening. But I am writing this in the shop, for I want to get it to the P.O. before today's mail goes out. I am sure it will amuse you. This morning about 10 o'clock, who should come through the door but Tom Gould.

He demanded to know "how Miss Lizzie is doing". He explained how he had come into the village to pick up the mail and how he just chanced to be going by and how he thought he'd stop in and inquire. I didn't ask him how he "just happened" to be so far off his usual track or why he was picking up his mail on Thursday when the newspaper isn't out until tomorrow. Well, anyway, he said he had written you several weeks ago and you had not replied. He asked me if I knew whether you had ever gotten his letter. I hemmed and hawed, but finally I told him the truth. I told him you were very upset about the darky living with him. He seemed provoked.

Then he said Jericho (I think that's the boy's name) was his business. He looked as if he planned to make some sort of an explanation, but apparently he changed his mind for he turned around and stalked out. Perhaps you can figure out the meaning of all this, but I would say that whether he knows it or not, Tom Gould is quite smitten with you.

I'll write you a longer letter some evening next week.

Emma

❈   ❈   ❈

A month later Tom wrote again:

Lisbon, Maine
Apr 16th, 1867

Dear Lizzie,

I hope you wont mind another letter from me, even if you didn't anser the last one I rote you. I spoke to your sister a wile ago and she said you was upset about Jericho. I want you to know that Jericho and me are good friends, even if he is just a boy, and I dont want to do anything to hurt him. I asked him if he would like to go to school and he said he would. So last night I rote a letter to that place in portland. I hope they anser my letter quicker than you did. I got the address from the Methodist deacon.

Things are about the same with me. Frank Farrar told me yesterday that Lil is in a family way. He expects to become a father sometime in August. Lil is doing fine. My mother is planning to stay with her when her time comes. She helps with a lot of birthings. I think about you a lot and wonder how your doing. How is your teaching going. Do you have good students. The GAR Post was finaly organized and we had our first meeting last week. Representative Jim Blaine was home from Washington and he came to our dedication. I shook hands with him. He is quite an orator. They say if the Republicans win next year, he might be Speaker of the House, and the way he is going someday he will probbly end up as President. He talked about buying Alaska from the Tzar of Russia. From what I herd, it sounded to me like buying the worlds biggest icebox without anything to put in it. If they just want to keep things cold, they could put them down my well, but he seemed to feel its a good skeme. I guess he knows what he is talking about.

I hope you like what Im doing about Jericho. Im going to miss him.

I offen think about you and would like to here from you.

Yr good friend,
Tom Gould

On April 20, Lizzie confided to her diary:

"I have been reading Ralph Waldo Emerson, a remarkable writer. He writes of Love: 'It is a fire that kindling its first embers in the narrow nook of a private bosom, caught from a wandering spark out of another heart, glows and enlarges until it warms and beams upon multitudes of men and women, upon the universal heart of all, and so lights up the whole world and all nature with its generous flames.' I believe I will memorize this."

The Rev. Caleb C. Foster wrote his sister from his new parish in the foothills of the White Mountains.

**The Methodist Parsonage
Northwood, New Hamp.
Fri., May 3, 1867**

My Dearest Sister Lizzie:

The crusading spirit still lives in the Foster family! I was so pleased for you when I read in your latest letter of the beneficial effect your Christian convictions have had on Mr. Gould. From what you tell me, this Jericho lad may well grow up to be a credit to his race. I am certain, also, that Mr. Gould will be eternally grateful to you for showing him the way of our Savior. How glorious it is when a good effort, such as your insistence that young Jericho receive Christian instruction, is productive and one discovers that one's words are not just a "vox clamantis in deserto". (Translation: "a voice crying in the wilderness"—Math. 3:3). I am not surprised that you are renewing your acquaintanceship with Mr. Gould, for certainly his recent change of heart demonstrates the Proverb that "He is in the way of life that keepeth instructions".

Have you written Jennie, our missionary sister, about your venture into (and success in) improving the condition of our black brothers? Perhaps you have seen her (since I understand she is back in Portland) and have been able to discuss with her your contre-temps with Mr. Gould. It will bring her lasting satisfaction to know that another is accomplishing in a small way that which she has set as her life's goal.

I am afraid there is still some question whether the Board will permit her to return to her beloved Harpers Ferry, where she was having such signal success. Many Secessionists still harbor rancor toward anyone dedicated to helping the Freedmen. They have not only made threats against Jennie but are also, I am afraid, spreading malicious gossip about her.

It is gratifying to be back in the spring weather again after the dreadful winter we have experienced. Not only have we had what seemed like weeks of below-freezing temperatures, but to have them last so far into the spring! It is now May and only in the last few days has the frost left the ground in the garden plot on the north side of the parsonage where I have been looking forward to cultivating so expectantly.

Yrs. in Jesus Christ
Your affectionate Bro.
Caleb

CHAPTER 10

On the night of May 14ᵗʰ, 1867, Tom had already said goodnight to his mother and Eunice and had gone up the back stairs to his bed chamber. Abruptly he reappeared in the kitchen doorway.

"I forgot to tell you Niah's comin' up in the mornin' to do the chores," he told his mother.

"Where you going to be?" she asked.

"Headin' into Portland. Before you get up. Be gone all day."

"You're not driving Fan all the way to Portland, be you? Must be fifty miles."

"Dhow. Just to Lewiston. Seven-thirty there's a steam train out o' Lewiston and another one comin' back from Portland about four o'clock in the afternoon."

"Do be careful, Tom. Those engines blow up, don't they?"

"Don't you worry about that. Uncle Sam and the Army took me on steam trains all over this nation and none of them's blowed up on me yet."

"Can't Jericho do the chores?" asked Eunice, looking up from her Bible. She was at the table reading by the dim light of a candle. "Niah's got his own chores to do down to his father's."

"Jericho's goin' with me. I spoke to Jake and he said he could spare Niah."

"You paying him?" Eunice asked.

"Of course, Tom's paying him," his mother replied before he had a chance to speak. "I declare, Eunice, sometimes I don't know what to make of you. Asking questions like that!"

"Well, it didn't seem to me as though Tom would pay if he could get the work done for free," Eunice explained—smiling at Tom, however, to take the sting from her remark. Rebecca frowned, but decided only to reroute the discussion.

"Why are you taking Jericho with you, dear? He follows you around, now, like a black shadow."

"I guess Jericho's goin' to school. I wrote to a place in Portland and they wrote back and said to bring him in and they'd learn him and then find him a job."

"Oh, Tom. That's wonderful!" his mother exclaimed. "How in the world did you find such a place?"

"Hank Waters give me the address. It's run by the Methodists."

"I'm so glad. How long have you been planning this?"

"Some weeks. Thought you might wonder why Niah was doin' the chores. Probably be dark by the time I get back tomorrow night." He started up the stairs a second time and pulled the door shut behind him.

"Well," said Eunice as the sound of his footsteps died away. "What do you make of that?"

"I've been wondering a long time what Tom's going to do about Jericho. Tom's not one to let you in on his thoughts."

"Well, I'm glad he's doing something. Having that little dusky heathen around here makes me uneasy. No telling what one of those folks is going to do."

"Why, Eunice. I never knew you felt that way. Jericho's so likable, it never dawned on me to be afraid of him."

"I'm not afraid, just uneasy. Every time I see him I think about that sea captain's family down to Pemaquid and that heathen child they took in."

"I don't believe I've heard that story."

"Oh, you certainly have. You remember the school teacher who boarded with us before Father passed on. He told about them."

"I guess I wasn't listening."

"Well, it has to do with a sea captain who brought back a baby he'd bought out in one of those heathen places sea captains end up in when they go around the world. I don't remember all the wherefores, but I guess it was because his wife couldn't have children of her own. Anyways, he bought this baby for her. Its mother had died or something, so they were selling it. Well, it turned out his wife was as pleased as she could be. So they adopted the little pickaninnny and took her into their home just like their own daughter. They bought her the best of everything, had her christened, even sent her to a private school. Except for her color, you'd never know she wasn't one of theirs. Then, when she was about eighteen she took sick. Doctors couldn't figure out what was the matter with her. She kept going down hill until at last everyone could see she was going to die."

"I think I remember hearing about this," Rebecca said, nodding. "What happened then?"

"The old captain went up to his daughter's bedroom, took her hand and asked her if there was anything he could get for her to make her comfortable. She shook her head. He pleaded. Wasn't there some kind of food that would taste good to her? Finally she said, Yes, she thought a roast baby's leg would taste good."

"Heaven's sake," Rebecca exclaimed. Eunice continued:

"Of course, the girl was out of her mind with fever. But it just goes to show. Once a savage, always a savage. No matter how much learning they get, it makes no difference. Sooner or later they throw back to their natures."

"Oh, Eunice. I can't believe that."

"Well, you can believe it or not, whatever you want. I'm just saying we're all better off letting the Methodists take care of Jericho. If he wants something special to eat, let them get it for him"

"Where'd you say this terrible thing happened?"

"Down to Pemaquid, I think he said. I guess that's an off port down the coast somewheres."

May 17th, 1867

My dear Lizzie,

I took Jericho to Portland last Tuesday and left him with a Mr. Dixon at the Methodist mission, just like you suggested. There going to learn him whatever he needs to know and then they will find a job for him afterwards. I'm going to miss the little cuss. We been comrades for a long time. I hope this means you will start riting to me again.

I asked after your sister Jennie whiles I was in there and they told me she had gone off to South Carolina to set up another school. Her name's Sarah Jane, they said. It took them quite a while to find her name. She's a real doer.

When you rite her tell her to be sure to take her quinine. Shes going to need it down there. Theres fever everywhere. Most everybody in my outfit got it.

My mother just asked me what I was riting and I said I was riting a letter to my friend Miss Elizabeth Foster to tell her that Jericho was going to school.

She says to send you her regards. And my sister Eunice sends hers.

Yr good friend,
Tom Gould.

❦   ❦   ❦

c/o Mr. Wordsworth Merrill
Poland, Maine
May 24, 1867

Dear Tom,

Thank you so much for your letter telling me about the boy Jericho. I am so happy to hear that he is getting a chance to make something of himself. We owe this opportunity to all the Negro children you and your comrades-in-arms fought so valiantly to free, and I am certain that our Heavenly Father has a special place in His heart for all who are helping them. Bless you, Tom Gould. I am so proud of you.

I am sending your advice about quinine to my sister in South Carolina. She will be very pleased to hear about little Jericho, for she is dedicated to bringing some light into the dismal lives of the former slaves. While she was home she told such uplifting stories of the nobility she has found in the hearts of these former downtrodden wretches.

I shall be teaching for only another month and then shall return to Gray and my family for the summer. My brother Howard is at home now. I expect he will be able to drive me to Lisbon to visit Emma. I suppose you have heard about Howard's ordeal in being released from the Army. Unfortunately, although the facts are much as they have been reported, the newspaper accounts have still been very distorted. Howard also suffered the ague just as you. After the surrender brought peace, he longed to come back to Gray where he could be properly cared for. But somehow his papers were misplaced (or perhaps even lost) and he was kept in camp even after all his fellows had been mustered out.

Despairing, he came home without permission and as you (and apparently everyone else) have certainly read by now was promptly arrested for desertion.

We were confident all along that he would be acquitted, but it has been a long process. Only last week he received an honorable discharge and is now at home. It will probably be many months before he will have recovered his health and his confidence. If we come to Lisbon this summer I hope you two will be able to meet for I am sure you have many experiences to share.

With highest regards
H. Elizabeth Foster.

CHAPTER 11

Lisbon, Maine
August 28, 1867

Dearest Father:

I didn't need to "inquire around" (as you suggested) to find out about Lizzie's current beguilement, Tom Gould. Auntie Rounds more than keeps me posted on the comings and goings of the Gould family. She is a close friend of Aphia Gould, Tom's step-sister, and since Tom and Lizzie took that walk together, we seldom sit down for a chat that Auntie does not recount the latest wisdom about the Goulds. By her account, Tom is an eminently dependable member of an eminently dependable family. He served gallantly in the War. He was wounded at Spottsylvania but Auntie believes it was minor, and he was briefly taken prisoner at Gettysburg. For a while he was hospitalized with camp fever, but I believe he fully recovered because he now works from dawn to dusk, keeping his farm as neat and tidy as a counterpane. When he worships, it is at the Free-Will Baptist Church. As far as I know, he owes no one. I have never heard anyone dispute this assessment.

He owns a large house on 200 acres with barns, sties, cribs, orchards and beehives where he lives with his mother and an elderly half-sister. His father had a number of children before his first wife died, but I guess most of them have moved from Lisbon. There are other Goulds in town, but except for Jake, Aphia's husband, and the half-sister, Auntie never mentions them. There is a stonemason named Steven Gould. I suspect he is a relation but I am not sure. When the father was in his seventies, he remarried and had another family. I have never met Rebecca, Tom's mother, but I understand she is a plain, good woman. Tom has a younger brother and if you hear any gossip about a Gould, you can be sure they're not talking about Tom but about Levi, the brother. He could hardly wait for Tom to get out of the Army, so he could head out. Before he left, according to Aphia, he told Jake that although he loved his mother, a healthy rooster could not be expected to stay cooped up with two broody hens.

I have met Tom several times, but I cannot say I really know him. I have also met Jake, but only when he brings Aphia in for a visit. The Gould womenfolk stay pretty close to home and none of them are Methodists. Tom is hardly a dandy. The first time I met him he was still wearing parts of his old uniform and he thinks nothing of coming into town in his farm clothes. I suspect he bought his first frock coat to take Lizzie to church, which he still wears each time he has called on her this summer. From its appearance, I would estimate these are the only times he has worn it. As you may expect, he brings with him an aroma of husbandry.

My friend, Lil Farrar, tells me that in the Army Tom used to keep his company entertained with comical stories. I find this hard to believe from what I have seen of him, but her husband, who served with Tom, insists it is true. If his stories amused soldiers, I suspect that many of them are coarse. Howard was verily infatuated with him. While Howard was here they spent a whole day wandering around the farm gossiping about the military life.

I am certain Tom is very fond of Lizzie. I gather from your letter that you also have observed in Lizzie, as I have, a more than ordinary reception of his attentions. I suspect she sees him as a noble and fearless Gideon. Although Tom Gould would not be my choice, Lizzie could certainly do much worse.

Lizzie tells me that Tom wants to come to Gray sometime to meet the rest of our family. I imagine she will be transmitting this information to you in the near future.

I hope this letter reassures you.

Give my love to Mamma. You already know of my love for you.

Emma Ann.

Just before noon on Saturday, October 26, 1867, Howard Foster was sitting in front of his father's cobbler's shop. His head was tilted against the back of his chair to catch the warm rays of the late morning sun, his cap pulled over his eyes. He wore a peaceful smile. Saffron leaves drifted around him from the maple at the corner of the building. He was not asleep, for he was peering from under the visor to watch the activity at the tavern next door and up and down the post road. A wagon was approaching along the highway from the east.

Suddenly, he sat up.

"Tom Gould," he cried, jumping to his feet. "What in tarnation are you doing in Gray?"

"Mornin', Howard. Figured maybe I'd come over and have a talk with your father." Tom threw the reins over the dashboard, and climbed down to the roadway, extending his hand. "Is he in the shop?"

"It's mighty good to see you, Tom," said Howard, grasping Tom's hand with both of his. "The old man's not here right now. He'll be back in a couple of minutes. I'm tending the shop while he's getting the church over there ready for services tomorrow. Here, Tom, sit down, while I get another chair." He thwacked the seat of the chair he had been sitting on; then stepped inside and brought out another. Tom remained standing, studying the church Howard had indicated.

"Sit down, Tom. Whacha hurry? You're not going anywheres. Sit down and make yourself comfortable. The sexton [he nodded toward the church] won't have time to talk till he gets through sweeping. After you've lived with him as long as I have, you'll learn he only takes on one thing at a time."

Tom fastened the reins to a rail near the entrance of the shop and patted Fan along the side of her neck. Then he sat.

"Am I glad to see you, Tom," Howard said. "Let me tell you. Recovering from a war isn't all it's cracked up to be. For a while there I thought Lizzie was going to give up teaching so's she could stay home and take care of me. Sometimes you just long for someone to talk to. How often I think about the visit Lizzie and I had with you last summer. It was like a thaw after a long cold spell."

"I was glad for your company. Not much chance on a farm to chew the rag with someone."

"Don't know how many times I've thought about those talks. Why, just now, as you were driving up. You might even of seen the smile on my face. I was thinking about the moose you told me about that mistook one of your cows for a lady friend. I didn't know whether to believe that story or not."

"It's gospel."

"How about that sow that got loose and knocked over the beehive? How's she doing?"

Tom chuckled.

"That took place years ago," he said. "That sow was bacon long before I joined up. Honey-cured bacon, you might say."

"Oh, Tom." Howard threw his head back and laughed heartily. Tom looked toward the church where nothing was stirring. There was time for a short yarn.

"I'll tell you one," he began. "The other side of Lisbon village there's an old coot who's got four grown sons, none o' them what you might call sharp as a needle. Last Monday the youngest one—the most half-baked of the litter—showed up in my dooryard leadin' a heifer. 'Papa wants you to service Dolly, this cow here,' he said, handin' me a dollar. 'Mind if I let the bull do it?' I asked him."

Howard roared.

"I led the cow into the pen and let ol' 'Shazzar out of the tie-up. The young squirt just shook his head as he watched 'Shazzar fulfill his obligations, his eyes opened up near as wide as the barn door. When it was over, I started to lead 'Shazzar back into the shed. The boy grabbed my arm. 'He seemed to like it,' he said. 'An' she seemed to like it. Here's another dollar. Let 'em do it again.'"

"Tom," Howard said finally, out of breath from laughing, "You made that up."

"No sir," replied Tom, reaching toward his pocket. "And I got the dollar right here to prove it."

Across the way at the church a door slammed and a man walked out of the shadows, slipping a black, broad-brimmed hat over his pink, bald head. His long beard glistened like polished silver in the sunlight. Under his left arm he carried a wooden box.

"Here comes Father now," Howard said, quickly regaining his composure. "Looks as if he's loaded down. Tomorrow's Communion Sunday. Probably bringing the cups home to get them ready."

Tom stepped into the street and met Mr. Foster half way. "Can I help you carry the box, Mr. Foster? It looks heavy."

"I've got it all right. It's just gormy. Who are you?"

"I'm Tom Gould and I've come to talk to you."

"Aye yes, my daughter wrote me you'd be coming. You know Emma Ann; she's Hannah Elizabeth's sister; runs the hat shop in Lisbon. Wait until I set this box down and I'll shake hands with you." He moved to the chair where Tom had been sitting and placed the box on it. He stretched his hand toward Tom. "Aye yes, Mr. Gould. What can I do for you?"

"I want to talk with you."

"Yes?"

"Can we talk inside?"

"Aye yes, Mr. Gould. You bring a chair with you so you'll have some place to sit down and I'll carry this." He picked up the box and started inside. Tom followed. At the door Mr. Foster turned to Howard. "And while I was gone were the unshod beating down the door seeking shoes?"

"Not a one," said Howard.

CHAPTER 12

After a prolonged courtship, Mr. Thomas J. Gould of Lisbon, Me. and Miss H. Lizzie Foster of Lisbon Falls, Me. were legally joined in marriage on Sunday, August twenty-third, 1869. The ceremony was performed by the Rev. George Plummer, Minister of the Gospel.

On that October day nearly two years earlier, when Tom had visited the cobbler's shop in Gray, Moses Foster had believed in his heart that Lizzie merited a more polished gentleman, but he had not withheld permission for Tom to court his daughter. However, he sought delay. He described the obligation, which he vowed Lizzie had accepted, to the children of the town of Poland, pointing out that she would not be free to pursue any distracting adventure until after the end of the school year. Tom had promised to observe this restriction.

Meanwhile, inspired by Sarah Jane's heroism and Caleb's insistent call for Christian sacrifice, Lizzie announced that she had resolved that as soon as her teaching duties were completed in the spring, she would volunteer for missionary work among the freedmen. She wrote "Dear Sister Jennie" in South Carolina asking for instructions. But Sarah Jane, certain that Lizzie was unready for such a strenuous life, replied only vaguely and tentatively. Thus for several months Tom's importuning for an immediate union was in vain, and Lizzie's response remained sufficiently encouraging to keep the spark alive.

The return of spring in 1868 brought an epidemic of yellow fever to South Carolina. Jennie came home as soon as her school closed for summer vacation, but it was too late. Six children came north with her, homes in Massachusetts having been obtained for them. Deck passage was all that was permitted for Negroes. Since Jenny felt it her duty to care for them, she was on deck a great deal. She reached home June 10th. Twelve days later she was taken sick and in three more had died from that frightful disease.

The summer of mourning that followed prevented Tom from wooing urgently, but his attendance at memorial services for Sarah Jane Foster in Gray and at the Portland headquarters of the Methodist Missionary Society convinced Lizzie of his devotion and, even more, of his worthiness.

Moses was also impressed. He had expected members of the Abolitionist societies, who had been so much in evidence during the War, to turn out in a drove to honor his daughter. Instead, he learned that most of those who had once championed the cause Sarah Jane had died for, now deemed the battle won. Saving the black brother was no longer stylish. The Abolitionists had turned to more popular issues, such as the war against Demon Rum or the punishment of the Confederate renegades. When Tom appeared at the sparsely attended memorial ceremony, Moses' gratitude was boundless.

Soon after the Portland services, Tom was again felled by his recurring malady. His mother administered her home remedies as she had during his previous attacks. Although this time there were neither chills nor fever, the massive pain in his right side and back lasted longer than ever before. Finally she called Dr. William McLellan, the village doctor. At first he was thoroughly baffled. But after thoughtful consideration (and the slice of green-apple-and-honey pie Eunice placed before him), he declared sagely:

"Camp fever appears in many disguises, sometimes attacking the liver. Beyond any doubt, Tom's illness is one of these permutations."

He told Rebecca to continue the quinine and castor oil and recommended that a mustard plaster applied to the chest would draw the congestion from the lungs. The next day, to the doctor's surprise but with his hearty approval, Tom began to rally, but he remained weak. Jake sent Niah up to take care of the chores.

After he recovered, Tom wrote Lizzie that his farm duties had kept him from writing to her sooner. He chose not to mention his infirmity.

Lizzie's letters to Tom insisted that she was still determined to become a missionary—but she wrote with diminishing enthusiasm.

Tom's replies, mustering as much passion as he was capable of, advised against it. At home Lizzie's mother, enumerating the manifold dangers, was constantly and tearfully begging her to reconsider. Actually, neither her mother's beseeching nor Tom's advice was necessary for the shock of Jennie's death had already convinced Lizzie. As soon as she could conscientiously announce her change of heart, she wrote Tom that in the fall she would be returning to teaching, if the position in Poland were still open.

My dear Lizzie,

It was mighty good news that you are not going to be a missionary. It may be as true as you say that the darkies need someone to show them the way, but I need you too. I wood miss you terrible if you was to go off to one of those secesh states. Let me tell you. Them folks down there would just as soon cut your throat as spit.

I just got back from talking with Jed Leighton. You remember him, he heads up the School Board here in Lisbon. He tells me they need a teacher pretty bad for the school down to the falls. I was thinking, if they don't have a place for you in Poland, maybe Jed would hire you here in Lisbon. When I mentioned your name, he said he remembered you. I hope you can come to Lisbon, because then I can see you more offen.

Things are going pretty good here on the farm. Don't know much about whats going on around down town, so I don't have any news for you but I guess things are quiet. I am to busy to get out and see fokes much, but I usually go to GAR meetings. It will be good to have you here in Lisbon because then I will have a topmost reason to go down town once in a while. Mother sends her regards

Yr True friend
Tom Gould

Lizzie did not delay taking the teaching job that was soon offered her in Lisbon. Later that fall she wrote in her diary:

"Wed., October 8, 1868

"Dear Diary:

"I do so miss my dear departed sister, Jennie—Sarah Jane. I could open my heart to her so much more than I can to anyone else, even to sister Emma. I guess, perhaps, it was because she was far away. Now I have only you, dear Diary, to talk to, but no matter how much I beg, you never answer me. You only listen. You do not console, you never offer advice, and you do not even scold or tease.

"If Jennie were only still here, I would be writing her about Tom Gould, asking her what I should do. Tonight he again asked me to marry him. He is such a splendid man, so handsome and so brave. He owns a large and prosperous farm. Since I have been teaching here at the Falls, he has been very diligent in courting me, sometimes stopping by to call on me as many as four times a week. We attend church every Sunday and sometimes evening meetings. I frequently permit him to hold my hand and tonight when he asked if he might kiss me, I assented. I must say, he behaved respectfully, even with reverence. I am certain that he would make a fine husband. Most young women would not hesitate to accept his offer. But he is not as cultivated a man as my father expects his daughters to marry. He reads only the newspaper. And, yes, the Bible. He is very familiar with the Bible, although he seems to read it more for entertainment than for instruction. I have been told that he was not a regular church goer until he started escorting me. In spite of his rough edges, I have grown very fond of him. And I must admit, I got considerable enjoyment this evening when he kissed me. I shall pray tonight for guidance."

Just before Christmas Lizzie agreed to marry Tom—not, however, she insisted with firmness, until spring and the end of school. He was overjoyed, but not so ecstatic that he forgot his spring responsibilities. He stipulated that he would not have time to get married until after he was through haying. That was how the August date was decided upon. It was better than three years since that first day when Franklin and Lillian introduced them.

❧   ❧   ❧

A few days before the wedding, Rebecca (taking advantage of a moment when Eunice was napping in her room) cautioned Tom that he should cherish Lizzie as he would a tender flower and treat her with gentle kindness. He promised but was uncertain what being gentle to a tender flower might entail. Gentleness was not an attribute that came easily to Tom.

He could not remember a time when he was so young that he was not striding across the fields or through the forest in the footsteps of Jacob, his pioneer father, listening to tales of heroic triumph over nature; of violent struggles with the Indians and against the seasons to wrest a home from the wilderness. From his father he had learned to slaughter hogs, fell trees, harvest honey, pluck fowl, swing a scythe, and break the ice in the pond so the livestock could drink. There was very little gentleness in old Jacob.

Long before Tom understood the purpose of the ritual, he had watched as his father brought old 'Nezzar forth from the tie-up, snorting and stomping, to board a cow awaiting eagerly in the service pen. Boars and rams accomplished their office before his callow eyes, their mates enduring the ferocity of the union with abounding patience. Roosters pursued unwilling hens about the poultry pen, pinning their squawking heads to the ground before straddling them. There was no gentleness in the barnyard.

Tom's only contact with the world beyond the farm had been through the violence of war. The base vulgarity of his comrades-in-arms had at first surprised and even disgusted him, but he soon learned, at least, to fit his conversation to their pattern. Their drunkenness and whoring repulsed him, for his father, in addition to instruction in agronomy and animal husbandry, had grounded him well in a sense of duty and the Ten Commandments. But nothing he heard from the soldiers in his Company or learned from watching their behavior modified his conviction that the connubial couch was the place for male dominance.

His younger brother Levi was the gentle one. As the baby of the family he had stayed with their mother and Eunice while Tom was shadowing their father around the farm. Levi knew more of picking beans than planting them. He had learned about women from women. When the girls of Lisbon and the surrounding communities heard the name Gould, it was Levi who came to mind rather than Tom. Tom had admiration and some envy for Levi's free spirit, but little understanding of its essence.

One of the first things Tom had done after being mustered out of the Army was to climb to the boulder high in the pasture where many times he had seen his aged father rest before heading home for supper. Below on the southern slope stood the split rock in whose cleft Jacob had crouched for protection when a tornado roared up from the valley and laid waste the ancient pines. Here Tom sat for a time in tribute to his progenitor, leaning his back, as his father had done, against the oak tree that had grown around the stone. Gentleness, Tom believed, came only with exhaustion.

Nor presently was his passion disposed toward gentleness. With the approach of the wedding he found himself preoccupied with the intensified yearning in his loins, a hunger ripened during the preceding months as he learned with regularity of Frank Farrar's progress into the arena of matrimony: engagement, marriage, honeymoon, pregnancy, and childbirth. In the name of friendship, Frank had felt bound to reveal the enchantment of each step to Tom. Tom's glands had responded.

On the morning of Monday, August 24th, the day after the wedding ceremony, Tom arose early, as was his custom, and headed for the barn to see about the chores. Rebecca and Eunice were soon in the kitchen, fetching water from the well in the cellar, wood from the shed beside the backdoor, eggs from the henhouse built against the south side of the barn. Later, Lizzie appeared.

"Good morning, Mrs. Gould," cried Eunice gaily.

"It's a lovely morning, Sister Eunice," Lizzie replied. "And what can I do to help, Mother Gould?"

When Eunice first spoke, Rebecca had looked up from the pork scraps she was frying and had noticed immediately that despite Lizzie's cheerful demeanor, her eyes were red and puffy.

BOOK TWO

CHAPTER 13

"In the last fifteen years I have had constant opportunity to practice what I have learned from many sources, and with the assistance and encouragement of some very able physicians.

*"I have evolved from my experience some theories which I think should go on record. Putting them to test, I have seen many puny half-starved babies speedily restored to health and happiness, and have had no contrary experience. **Science of Feeding Babies and Normal Care of the Growing Child** for nursing-mothers and infants' nurses: H. Elizabeth Gould. Rebman Company, NY. (1916) Pg. 2.*

"There you be, Lizzie," Aphia panted. "I mighta knowed I'd 'a' found you workin'. Married less than a month, and already you're grubbin' out in the garden just like a regular Gould woman."

The elderly sister-in-law had just walked from her home up the path through the orchard and climbed the terraces that ascended to the dooryard of the old farmhouse. Along the way she had gathered in her apron the apples she found lying under the trees. She paused to catch her wind, steadying herself against one of the maples that lined the margin.

"This isn't work," Lizzie laughed. "I'm just gathering dill for Mother Gould's pickles...Are you all right?" she asked with concern as Aphia sighed and took a deep breath.

"Fine. Just a dite winded. That's a real climb for an old lady. Picked up these windfalls along the way to save Eunice the trouble." She fanned herself with her free hand and lifted the front of her dress to let the air circulate around her breasts.

"When I came out the door a few minutes ago," Lizzie said, "and saw you coming up the path, I thought: I do hope Aphia's coming to sit awhile. We haven't seen you for what seems like an age."

"Figured it wouldn't do no harm to neighbor a bit."

"Not a bit," Lizzie agreed eagerly.

"Farm life must be gittin' pretty lonesome for you, ain't it?" Aphia asked.

"Not at all. I'm too busy to be lonely. But it is pleasant to speak with some-one different now and then."

"That's just what I figured. I kind o' guessed that after the first week 'Becca and Eunice would run out o' things to talk about, cooped up the way they be in this old house."

"Mother Gould's been teaching me so many new things, the days go by fast, indeed."

"Tom's prob'ly just like Jake. Works from dark to dark and then's too worn out to do anything but fill his craw and climb inta bed. I been worried about you, Lizzie. You ain't used to life on a farm. You need to git out."

"Why, Aphia. Aren't you kind to think about me?"

"I come up, mainly, to see if you'd want to go to a sewin' session over to Bess Sturdevant's tomorrow. I know it's just a waste a time to ask the two old women if they want to go. Oh, I'll ask 'em. I always do, but I know already what they're goin' to say. Too busy. Always too busy. But you ain't 'customed to this life, Lizzie."

"I'd love to go, but I'll have to ask Tom. He's had a severe pain in his side all morning and has been in bed."

"In bed? What's he gut this time? The camp fever again?

"I'm afraid so. There's some jaundice. Tom thinks it has settled in his liver."

"I figured Tom's fever was back when I seen Niah comin' down the back way. Guessed he must of been helpin' with the chores. But let me get free o' these apples, Lizzie. Whilst I visit with the old women, you go ask Tom."

"'Old women'. What a thing for you to say, 'Phia."

"Well, I may be jest as decrepit as they be, but I do make an effort to git out o' the house every once in a dog's age. Now, skedaddle, and don't let Tom talk you out o' goin'."

❧   ❧   ❧

Lizzie was not as unaccustomed to farm life as Aphia suggested. Although the home where she grew up was located within the village of Gray, it nevertheless sat on a parcel of land that stretched back several hundred feet from the highway. When her father, Moses, was not making shoes in his shop or tidying up the two churches he served as sexton, he could usually be found cultivating a large garden. During her childhood, he had always kept poultry in the pen at the rear of his property, and some years he had even raised a pig in the sty adjoining the chicken coop. All the children spent many hours weeding and hoeing the rows of vegetables in their father's garden and it was the special duty of the girls to feed the chickens and pick up the eggs.

A neighbor owned several milch cows, and Lizzie could not remember a time when one of her brothers was not helping care for these animals in exchange for a daily bucket of milk and an annual supply of "cow dressing" for their father's garden. Caleb began teaching Lizzie to milk a cow shortly after she learned to walk. Being a cobbler may have produced only a meager livelihood, but Moses always saw to it that his family had food on the table and books to read.

He kept his daughters strictly isolated from the tavern next door to his shop, and particularly from the vulgar, even bawdy, discussions among the hands at the livery stable nearby. He considered it especially fortunate that in 1858 while his children were still young, the State of Maine had enacted, with his enthusiastic support, a stringent prohibition law. They were thus spared exposure to the evils of rum.

Nevertheless, the excitement of the village permeated his children's lives. It was impossible to conceal the bustling activity that resulted when the stages arrived at the tavern, particularly if an individual of prominence was aboard and he took food or refreshment while the horses were being exchanged. Frequently the Foster girls and their young friends created "accidental" excuses to be in the neighborhood when these dramatic moments occurred.

Lizzie's mother was a cousin of Meschach Humphrey, a prominent Maine politician and the State Senator from Cumberland. Frequently, on his way to and from the State Capitol at Augusta he stopped at the Foster home, for he enjoyed talking with Moses. More than once he had been accompanied by other officials and personages whose fame extended well beyond the boundaries of Maine.

Generally, the Foster children were their own entertainment. Before Caleb had gone off to the seminary in Lewiston he was forever conceiving Biblical tableaux and requiring his siblings to perform in them. Many times he insisted that it was Lizzie's turn to be thrown into the lion's den or to stand motionless as a pillar of salt or to enact similar feats as part of his pageantry. Jennie discovered after Caleb left that she was equally as imaginative as her brother. Emma and Lizzie were not far behind.

Particularly during the long winter evenings Moses—to amuse and instruct his family—gathered his children about him and asked them to describe what they had read or discovered that day. Sometimes he read aloud. Books were not common in Gray, but sooner or later almost any respectable reading matter that appeared in town found its way into the hands of the Fosters.

Since Lizzie had assumed that most homes were like hers, the prosaic day-to-day existence in the Gould household came as a shock to her. Eunice with her flower garden did produce occasional displays of beauty. Both Tom and his mother demonstrated flashes of humor. But Lizzie had to supply her own sense of discovery, her own enthusiasm, her own creative imagination. She didn't feel lonely, for there was much genuine love in the home and plenty of work to keep her mind and hands busy. Although she wouldn't admit it, she knew Aphia was right in saying that Lizzie was not accustomed to this life.

Tom was lying in bed looking at the ceiling when Lizzie whispered outside his closed door:

"Are you awake, Tom, dear?"

"Ayuh, come on in, Lizzie. I'm feelin' better. I was just about to get outa bed and put my pants on. I guess I must of gone off to sleep when the pain let up…What've you been up to all mornin'?"

"Helping around the house. I tried to help Niah with the chores," she laughed in self-deprecation, "but I guess I wasn't much use. There's so much I don't know about barn work."

"Don't you worry 'bout that, my darling wife. It's not hard to get the drift of farmin' once you get into it. Anything you need to know, I can learn you."

"I expect you to teach me everything about the farm, Tom. There is so much we can learn from each other."

Tom laughed.

"Lizzie, dear, I guess it's goin' to be harder for you to teach me to talk right, than it'll be for me to learn you to feed the hogs."

"Don't tease, now, Tom. 'Phia's here and she wants to know whether I would like to drive over to Bessie Sturdevant's with her tomorrow. They're having some sort of a sewing bee."

"Of course, why shouldn't you go?"

"I just thought that perhaps since you've been sick all day, you'd need me here."

"Lizzie, there's always work on the farm, but if you want to go with 'Phia, you go right ahead. I'll git along all right, I guess. There'll be plenty of work still here when you get back."

"If you don't want me to go, Tom, dear, I won't mind."

"Well, me bein' sick has put us behind."

"I'll just tell Aphia to remember me next time."

CHAPTER 14

"Nature, with all her marvelous skill, has never produced a fairer picture than a dimpled, laughing baby. All healthy babies spontaneously develop into the laughing and dimpled kind, and the chief ingredient to that natural development is a sufficiency of proper food." **Science of Feeding Babies and Normal Care of the Growing Child for nursing mothers and infants' nurses:** *H. Elizabeth Gould. Rebman Co. NY (1916) Pg. 5*

"Mother Gould," Lizzie remarked, straining to lift a heavy bucket of water to the drainboard. "Wouldn't it be convenient to have a pump here in the kitchen sink? Then we wouldn't have to go down cellar to get water."

"Yes…I suppose it would." Rebecca replied. "Tom's father mentioned it before he passed on, but he never did get around to it. Levi said he was going to do something about it, but then he left. Jericho used to bring the water up for us before he went off to school."

"I'll ask Tom."

"I should think Tom has enough on his mind," Eunice interrupted, "Without being bothered with kitchen problems."

"Jake has installed a pump for Aphia in her sink," Lizzie asserted.

"Yes, I know," Rebecca agreed. "It was when Jake put Aphia's pump in that Levi and his father were talking about getting one for us."

"Was it much of a chore? Putting it in, I mean."

"Much of a chore!" Eunice sniffed. "Tom would have to rebuild this whole kitchen. The well's away over there—under that corner—clear across the kitchen from where the sink is now. I like the sink just where it is, right by this window."

"Tom could move the sink over to the other window. The well's directly underneath. We could still look out."

"I just don't know," sighed Rebecca.

"I'm going to ask Tom," Lizzie said.

"I don't know," was Tom's response. "I suspect a pump'd be pretty expensive. What do you think, Mother? Do you need a pump?"

"Well, I've got along all these years without one, but I guess it'd be handy."

"It'd take several days to install it," Eunice declared, "Away from your chores. You've got to consider that, Tom. But then, it means nothing to me. I don't spend much time anymore at the sink anyway. If Lizzie wants it, it's all right with me. Nobody asked my opinion when Father was talking about it."

"I'll think about it, Lizzie," Tom said. "I'll ask what a pump costs when I go into town."

The bedroom where Tom and Lizzie slept was on the southeast corner of the second floor of the great, square farmhouse. Rebecca and Eunice had separate bedrooms just off the kitchen and behind the parlor on the first floor. Lizzie had soon learned that privacy was possible only after she and Tom had retired.

It was the third of November, 1869, a few days after she had broached the subject of a pump.

"Tom, dear," she said softly as he climbed into bed beside her.

"Yes, Lizzie."

"You promised to investigate the cost of a pump for the kitchen."

"I already did. They're dear."

"Jake got their pump for a half bushel of corn."

"Where'd you hear that?"

"That's what Aphia said."

"Huh…Well, we'll see."

There was silence for a few minutes as he reached over and began to fumble with the folds of her chemise, slowly raising the hem as he nuzzled against her collar bone.

"Tom," she spoke again; this time in a tone of mild defiance. "I must have a pump in the kitchen."

"I told you: I'll see about it."

"I must have your promise that you shall get me a pump."

"I can't get it tomorrow."

"I don't know why not. You said yourself: this time of year a farmer doesn't have much to do except get ready for another season. My pump falls in that category."

"What's the fuss? Mother's been carrying water up from the cellar all her married life. A lot of women have to go outdoors to get water. Over in Gray your own family has an outside well."

"Tom, my darling, your mother is getting too old to be carrying a heavy pail of water up that flight of stairs."

"Aye, yes."

"And Eunice is already too old," Lizzie added.

"Eunice ain't carried water upstairs since she was a girl. Why should she start now?"

"Well then, who do you expect will be lugging water when my condition no longer allows me to lift heavy objects?"

"That ain't going to be tomorrow, be it?" Tom's hand was still exploring. He lifted his face to kiss his wife's cheek and tasted the saltiness of tears.

"Why, Lizzie," he said. "You ain't crying about an old pump? You've got to realize there may be a lot of things we can't get along without, but your pump's pretty far down on the list."

Lizzie did not reply. She reached down to move his hand off her leg. She caught her breath in a sob.

Suddenly, a single word of the previous conversation reverberated in Tom's mind.

"Condition!" he cried. "Lizzie, you ain't in a condition, be you?"

By the time Ralph Ernest Gould was born in Rebecca's bedroom on July 14, 1870, Eunice, as well as the other women in the household, had become proficient at drawing water with the new pump. During the birth she was kept busy heating water on the stove and bringing basins of it to Rebecca as they were required. Lizzie had wanted Dr. McLellan to attend her, but when she complained to Aphia that Tom had said he didn't plan to call the doctor, she was assured that she couldn't do better for a midwife than to depend on her mother-in-law.

"'Becca's got more knowledge about yarbs and nature's remedies than any Injun you ever seen," Aphia said. "For that matter, I guess she learnt most of it straight from the Redskins. There's a whole mess of them still living down there nearby where she and the other Hinckleys was brung up. You'll get along just fine, dearie, with 'Becca looking out for you."

Lizzie had come down to the kitchen shortly after midnight because she couldn't sleep. The July heat was oppressive. She was apprehensive lest her restlessness disturb Tom. Flashes of lightning lit the sky far off to the east as a summer storm followed the Kennebec River to the sea. Patches of moonlight on the floor were the only other illumination. She was nibbling on a hardtack she had found in a bin near the pantry when she felt the first pain. She was not sure. She waited for a second and third. She had no timepiece, but she estimated they were at least ten minutes apart. The clock in the hallway near the front door had struck "one" and then struck "one" again. Was it one o'clock or one-thirty? The next pain was extraordinarily sharp. She knocked on Rebecca's door.

"Shall I wake Tom?" she asked.

"Let Tom sleep. He'd just be underfoot. You stretch out on my bed and I'll get Eunice. Here, now...I'll light this candle...Let me straighten out the covers...There, now. You just make yourself as comfortable as you can and I'll be right back. Everything's going to be all right."

When Tom appeared in the kitchen shortly before sun-up, Eunice greeted him with:

"You'll just have to get your own breakfast this morning, Tom Gould."

"Where's Lizzie? I woke up and she wan't in bed. Where is she?"

"She's in your mother's chamber."

Tom started for the door, which was ajar, but Rebecca stopped him before he could enter.

"We don't need you in here, Tom. You go do your chores."

"Where's Lizzie? Is she all right?"

From the bed against the wall across the room, Lizzie groaned.

"She's doing fine," Rebecca insisted. "It'll only be a few more minutes."

Tom paced in the kitchen, until Eunice told him to go do his chores and get out of her way. Then he paced back and forth along the pathway to the barn. The sun rose, painting swatches of flame on the clouds that stretched along the horizon. Several times through the open windows he heard Lizzie cry out in pain. Then all was silent, except for the crows cawing to herald the dawn.

"Why don't you come in now, Tom, and see your son?" Eunice called from the doorway.

❦   ❦   ❦

Tom hardly knew what to expect. He had overseen many births in the barn. Only a few months before Fan had foaled for the second time. But this was the first time that it was not his responsibility to clean up the blood and afterbirth. He was relieved to find Lizzie smiling, dressed in fresh attire, lying on a clean sheet, holding in her arms a baby wrapped in a white blanket. It's small red face was almost all nose. Tom stood speechless for a moment at the foot of the bed, beaming with pride as he rubbed his hand over his beard. Then he moved up beside his wife and took her hand.

"Lizzie," he said, almost passionately.

"Tom, dearest, meet Ralph Emerson Gould."

"Ralph Emerson?" he asked in surprise. "Where'd you ever get ahold of a name like that?"

"Isn't he magnificent, Tom? Wouldn't it be fitting to name him after America's greatest writer, Ralph Waldo Emerson? I want my baby to grow up to be famous, a philosopher, perhaps."

"I don't know, Lizzie," said Tom, shaking his head. "I been considering Ernest as a real good name for a boy."

"You could call him Ralph Ernest," Rebecca suggested, beaming ecstatically at the happy couple and her first grandson. "He'd have the same initials that Lizzie wanted."

"That's a good idea," Eunice agreed, watching from the doorway. "Ralph Ernest, it shall be."

🍁   🍁   🍁

July 20, 1870

Dear Emma:

Just a note to thank you for the baby things you sent & to tell you what a handsome nephew you have. All went well & Ralph Ernest arrived on schedule. Everyone has been so good to us. Several neighbors also brought us clothing & Sister Aphia has given me a gown she was no longer using that she took in & shortened for me. I look quite grand as I sit in the window in my new dress rocking my precious son.

I had hoped to have Dr. McLellan attend me, but the whole family insisted that I needed no more than Mother Gould. It seems they were correct for everything went fine. Between Mother Gould and Sister Eunice I am being taken care of—perhaps too well. Sometimes, I have to go off by myself just to catch my breath. You can have no idea what it is like to live with two other women, both of whom were once the mistress of the house. Eunice and Tom's mother have made some sort of a truce over the years, but neither seems to have any desire to yield any control to the newcomer. When I try to make changes, one or the other, & sometimes both, tells me how Tom wants it. Even the baby's name was taken out of my hands, when they all decided that Ralph Ernest was preferable to Ralph Waldo Emerson. When I suggested to Tom that sometimes I feel useless, he laughed at me & quoted the Proverb about living with a brawling woman in a wide house. But that is neither here nor there, I am well taken care of and happy with my babykins.

When Father and Mother came to see the new baby, they brought Eliza with them and she visited with me for several days, but you probably already know about that. She's such a sweet child. The last time I really spent time with her was at least 5 years ago when she was only 6 or 7. It's sad not to know a dear sister better. She tells me that she wants to be a nurse and that Brother Avery has promised to help her become one, after he finishes medical school. I am so happy for her, that she shall have the opportunity that I wish I had had.

But I must not say that, for I now have a precious son.

Thanks again from your sister Lizzie.

CHAPTER 15

"Nothing has a greater power to waste the nerve force of our women than the present style of living. To copy as nearly as possible the homes of the wealthy, and to accomplish, without help, what the rich attempt with servants, is a too common ideal." **Science of Feeding Babies etc.:** *H. Elizabeth Gould. Rebman Co. NY (1916) Pg. 3*

Frank Farrar pulled his carriage to a stop before the wide front entrance of the Gould farmhouse. The lilac bushes on either side were only beginning to bloom but already the aroma filled the dooryard. The geranium roots that had wintered in the cellar were sending up shoots where Eunice had transplanted them into the narrow garden lining the edge of the terrace, and her rosebushes beneath the windows were covered with the fresh, green leaves of spring.

His wife Lil, with their new baby in her arms, waited as he tied the horse to the hitching post and positioned himself to help her get out. As she descended from the carriage, their older child scrambled down from the rear seat.

Lizzie opened the door.

"I heard you driving into the yard," she greeted. "Come on in. How good of you to stop by."

"Since you folks weren't to church this morning," Frank explained, "We figured we'd better inquire."

"Is anybody sick?" asked Lil.

"Tom's been a bit under the weather and since Mother Gould is over with Delia Hilton until her baby comes we decided not to go to church this morning."

"Don't tell me Tom ain't going to be fit to march on Tuesday," Frank demanded as he followed Lil into the parlor.

"He says he will be," Lizzie replied, more than a hint of annoyance in her tone. "Ask him yourself. You'll find him in the kitchen."

Frank crossed toward the kitchen, nodding a hello to Eunice who was sitting near the window, her Bible open in her lap, gently rocking with her foot the cradle in which baby Ralph was sleeping. As he left the room Lil was saying:

"I didn't realize Delia's time was so close."

The kitchen was substantial, fifteen by twenty feet. Pineboards, most of them a good deal more than a foot wide, ran the length of the floor. At the center of the inside wall stood a fieldstone fireplace with a broad slab of granite for a hearth. But its brick lining was dusty with disuse. In front of it was an iron cooking range with a stovepipe leading into a chimney hole just above the mantel. Tom was sitting in a rocking chair with his feet resting on the nickel trim of the cook stove. Despite the heat of the room—a kettle was steaming on the stove—his shoulders were wrapped in a shawl.

"The fever again?" Frank asked.

"Ayuh."

"Tain't going to keep you down for Tuesday, be it?"

"I should say not. 'Twouldn't do to miss Tuesday."

"Talked to Horace after church. He said he got the G.A.R. proclamation in the mail last Monday right from headquarters, from General Logan himself. Every year from here on out, May 30's going to be Decoration Day in honor of us veterans. Horace got the parade route all laid out for us. Hits every graveyard in town."

"Where do we meet?"

"Town Hall at nine o'clock."

"Everybody going to be there?" Tom asked.

"Far as I know."

"It'll be great to be together again."

"Sure will be."

❦   ❦   ❦

This was the second day that Tom had hunched over the stove. On Saturday he had been up as usual before dawn, but halfway through his chores he had returned to the kitchen to tell Lizzie that he was "all in" and that she would have to finish up for him. The baby was nestled against her breast, but she had risen to her feet when Tom entered. Immediately, he caved into the rocking chair she vacated. He listed the tasks that were left to be done.

"The animals will just have to wait until I finish feeding Ralph," she said.

"Don't take too long," he directed.

"You can't hurry Ralph."

"He won't take all day, will he?" Lizzie ignored his question.

"Don't you think you'd better go back to bed and get a good rest," she suggested.

"I'll just set here for a bit."

In a few minutes, Ralph turned his mouth away from his mother and she asked Eunice to care for him while she tended to the barn work. After the old woman had gathered the infant into her arms, Lizzie stroked Tom's forehead.

"Don't you believe I'm sick?" he asked peevishly.

"Of course, dear. I was just checking to see how much fever you have."

"I got plenty."

"You seem quite cool right now."

"I don't feel cool," he snapped, placing his hand above his hip. "Anyways, the pain in my gut's real enough—right here."

"Wrap this shawl over your shoulders, dear." She lifted the fringed garment from the back of the chair. "Here, sit up, I'll adjust it for you…"

"My gut hurts worse when I set up."

"Please, Tom, remember we have to be constantly thinking about our son. I don't believe 'gut' is a word we would want him to learn."

"That's where the misery is."

Lizzie smiled tolerantly.

"'Inwards' is a much more agreeable word, Tom. 'Intestines' would be less vulgar, but perhaps inaccurate. The best word is 'inwards.'"

Tom leaned back in the chair.

"Hens've got innards," he groaned.

Monday morning Tom appeared to be better. He fed the stock and finished the morning chores but then worked only until noon, turning over a strip of land in the upper meadow where the yellow-eye beans for the next winter's baking would be planted.

"If I try and plow any more today," he told Lizzie after he had returned the oxen to the tie-up, "I don't know whether my back'll let me march tomorrow. The beans can wait."

"Whatever you think best, Tom."

He retired to the bedroom upstairs.

Tuesday morning, the barn work was finished in short order.

"Ready to go?" he called to Lizzie as he brushed down his uniform. "Fan's all hitched up. It'll be the first time she's been out since she foaled."

"We're ready," Lizzie replied, "but I've been wondering. Do you think Ralph should be exposed to so much sun? It'll be a long day."

"He's got to see his father march."

"Yes, indeed. But I was thinking of the bivouac afterwards. How long is that going to last?"

"Probably till dark. They'll be lots of families there. Everybody'll want to see what the Gould family's produced." He patted Ralph on the back and chuckled.

As Tom started to drive out of the dooryard, the mare balked and looked back toward the barn.

"What's the matter now, Fan?" he asked softly.

"Probably she doesn't want to leave her baby," Lizzie suggested.

He leaned forward and spoke gently to the obstinate animal:

"Is that your trouble, old girl? Just can't bring yourself to leave Tantrabogus behind, eh?" He slapped the reins on her back but she didn't budge.

"Tantrabogus!" Lizzie exclaimed. "Where in the world did you get such a dreadful name?"

"Sounded like a good name for a horse," he replied, laughing.

"Can't Tant..." she paused and smiled as she stumbled over the name, "the colt come along with her mother?"

"Couldn't keep up."

"Perhaps if we drive slowly?"

"Is that what you want, old girl?" said Tom, speaking again to Fan. "To make us late for the parade."

"I declare," said Lizzie. "I believe she's nodding her head."

"Probably she is," agreed Tom. "She's a smart one."

He climbed down and let Tantrabogus out of the stable. Over her shoulder Fan watched as her offspring bounded to her side. The wagon proceeded slowly to the village with the colt wobbling alongside on his spindly legs.

"By-God-you-mister, here's Tom Gould, at last," Horace Jordan hollered from the center of a group of uniformed veterans standing in front of the town hall. "Farrar said you could be down with a case of the colic."

"It'd take more than colic to keep me down today," Tom called back, striding toward his friends. He had left Lizzie and the baby with the cluster of women gathered in the shade of the horse shed, where he had tied Fan with a generous forkful of hay scattered before her. As he had walked away, he patted the rump of Tantrabogus, who was now nuzzling against its mother's flank.

"Greetings and salutations," Tom exclaimed as he grasped Horace's outstretched hand.

"Here's a fellah you've got to watch every minute, by-God-you-mister," Horace announced to the group, emphasizing his profanity with a hearty guffaw. "Every minute, I say! Whatcha trading today, Tom?"

"Hain't trading nothing, you old coot, till I find out what kind of flummery you're offering."

"How about trading that fine-looking colt?"

"Not on your life. I plan to keep him."

"Plan to keep him, you say?" Still pumping Tom's hand, Horace spoke to the men surrounding them. "Don'tcha believe a damn word of it, by God. If Tom Gould brings a shoe lace 'round for folks to see, by-God-you-mister, he's looking for a trade."

"And unless Tom Gould's a bigger fool than I know him to be," Tom said to his fellow veterans, "He won't likely be making any horse trades soon with Horace (by God) Jordan."

"Then, by God, I guess I'm safe," said Horace, mopping his forehead in mock relief.

"I wouldn't count on it," Tom threatened jovially and all the men joined in the laughter.

"Here comes Judge Jack," someone announced near the edge of the group. "Just like the cow's tail."

"Don't let him hear you say that," another replied, "or he'll speechify for an hour on the virtues of tardiness. He's supposed to ride in the carriage with Preacher Plummer right back of the flag bearer."

"Now, there's a rare pair of speechifiers for you. Whichever one starts first, t'other one won't get a word in edgewise."

"We ain't going to stand to attention while they're holding forth, be we, Horace?" asked a tall fellow at the rear of the group. They all laughed except Horace.

"By-God-you-mister," he said, ignoring the questioner, "if the Judge's here, guess we're ready to move out."

He called over to the ladies and several of them broke away from the group, bringing bouquets of flowers for the veterans to carry: lilacs and peonies, and even some tulips that Susan Curtis had found still blooming against the northwest side of her house. The drums began and the former soldiers with serious mien—some with tears on their cheeks—started the solemn march to the cemeteries to decorate the graves of fallen comrades.

CHAPTER 16

"We may begin very early to interest children in scientific facts about their own bodies. If we are able to state any truth in an interesting manner, we shall find that we have an unfailing fund of entertainment for them.

The allegory of the little workmen will claim and hold the attention of any child who is old enough to appreciate the hurt of a scratch or cut, which brings the blood.

A kiss will cure many a hurt, but when the skin is broken, mother or nurse bathes the place and binds it up with a strip of clean linen, while she says cheerily, "Now the little workmen will have to mend this." **Science of Feeding Babies etc.** *H. Elizabeth Gould. Rebman Co. NY. (1916) Pg. 109*

Lisbon, Maine
May 30, 1871

My dearest Sister Emma:

Everybody at the parade this morning was asking for you. Auntie Rounds showed me the letter she received from you last week and insisted I read every word of it, even though it was very like the letter you sent me the week before.

She's such a dear, sweet lady and she misses you so much since you have departed "from her hearth and home". She joins me in hoping that as soon as you are able to travel you will come visit us, bring the baby and stop by to see her. New Gloucester is not so far distant and I am sure that the new father and mother are both looking forward to showing off the latest addition to the Thompson family. You sound so happy in your new home.

Lisbon's first Decoration Day observance was very successful. The men of the G.A.R. had erected a platform in front of the Town Hall and adorned it with bunting. The Rev. Mr. Plummer gave his usual laudable invocation and the Hon. Mr. Jack delivered an eloquent eulogy. Music for the marching was provided by several young men and boys who have organized a fife and drum corps. Several wives were discussing forming a Relief Corps so that by next year's Decoration Day the women can prepare dinner and serve it under the maples.

Tom looked so very fine in his uniform as he marched with his outfit. You would recognize the names of a number of the men who were in the parade, but I will not attempt to make a list of them. I was grateful that the Farrars were there, because after the parade it became very hot and Lil generously offered to bring Ralph and me home when she left early with her two young-sters. Tom stayed on to be with his comrades. I had made him a "ham sand-wich", as they say, and left it for him in a basket in the wagon, so he hasn't gone hungry. I am writing this as I wait for him to come home. Mother Gould is staying over with Delia Tuttle, who is expecting her fourth child; and Sister Eunice is resting in her room.

A marvelous incident, which I am sure will delight you, occurred on the way to the parade. Our mare Fan, who foaled only last week, absolutely refused to leave the dooryard without her colt.(I won't attempt to spell the name Tom dreamed up for said colt.) When Tom asked her if she wanted to take the colt with her, she nodded just as if she knew what he was saying. So Tom, who is so caring with his animals, let the colt run alongside even though it made us a lit-tle late. Motherhood is such a powerful force.

It has cooled off now here on the Ridge. A nice breeze is blowing up from the river. The weather, as you know, has been unusually warm for this time of year. Tom had a bad spell Sat. and Sun. so I had to do much of the barn work as well as take care of Ralph and do the cooking. It's been particularly hard in all the heat. Eunice tries but at her age she's not really very much help. I miss Mother Gould when she's away. She insists Ralph's a fussy baby because he wakes up in the night and cries, but he's my little angel.

I thank you so much for sending me "The Minister's Wooing." I had not read it. I shall return it as soon as I have finished. Last month Father loaned me Mrs. Stowe's more recent novel, "The Pearl of Orr's Island," which I enjoyed very much, but I had not seen this earlier book of hers until you sent it to me. She is such a noble writer, constantly interrupting her narrative to draw a significant moral. We have so little reading matter in this house. I don't know what I would do without my generous family.

We must count our blessings and thank the Good Lord.

Your affectionate sister,
Lizzie.

❦   ❦   ❦

"Did you ever hear from that darky boy you brought home with you after the War, Tom?" Eunice asked at the kitchen table one evening as the family was finishing supper. "Up in my room this afternoon I got to wondering whatever happened to him."

"You mean Jericho?"

"Was there any other boy you brought home with you?"

Tom ignored the sarcasm in his half-sister's question.

"Got a letter from him a month or so ago."

Lizzie, who was sitting nearby in the rocking chair nursing Ralph, looked at Tom in bewilderment.

"You never told me you'd heard from Jericho."

"Didn't think you'd be interested."

"Of course, I'm interested. How is the child doing?"

"He ain't much of a child these days. He's shoveling coal down to the Portland waterfront."

"I'm so glad he's had such an opportunity to find solace in the Lord," Lizzie said. "He seemed like such a promising young fellow. Did he sound happy?"

"Guess so. Happy as anybody shovelin' coal for a living could be. Signed his letter, 'Gerald Dixon'. Pretty fancy name he took for himself, I'd say."

"I would say it's a fine name. Could I see the letter?"

"Dhow. Hain't got it now. Don't know what I did with it. Probably stuck it up behind a post in the barn. If I find it." He paused and pushed back his chair before asking: "What in tarnation do you want to see it for?"

"I'm just interested in how the boy turned out. I might write him and tell him how proud we are."

Eunice rose abruptly from the table and started carrying dishes to the sink.

"I don't see why Lizzie should be interested," she commented to Tom, almost as if Lizzie were absent. "She never knew him."

"I met him the first day I ever came to the farm," Lizzie corrected in a gentle voice. Mother Gould interrupted:

"I believe Lizzie suggested the mission in Portland where Tom took little Jericho to get some learning."

"Maybe she did and maybe she didn't," Tom growled as he abruptly left the table and climbed the back stairs to the bed chamber.

CHAPTER 17

"It will be a great help toward the best results if young people have not married until a sufficient income is assured to meet reasonable expenses, and they can lay by a certain amount each week for an emergency fund." **Science of Feeding Babies etc.:** *H. Elizabeth Gould. Rebman Co. NY. (1916) Pg. 85*

One morning several weeks later, perhaps a few minutes after seven, Lizzie heard a rap on the back door. Tom was already in the field; Rebecca was at her loom in the open chamber at the rear of the second floor—before the midday heat would drive her back to the cooler rooms on the first; Eunice had returned to the sanctuary of her bedroom with some mending she said required attention; baby Ralph was walking about the kitchen with his hands in the air, demonstrating—for his mother's delight and his own evolving ego—a recently discovered use for his feet and legs. Lizzie gathered the baby in her arms and headed for the door.

"Who is it?" she called.

"Big-John Coombs with Rebecca's wool," a voice replied. The Coombses of Lisbon were prolific, especially in producing males. And their affinity for the name John was notorious. Besides Big-John Coombs, there were: Short-John, Fat-John, One-eye-John and Two-thumb-John as well as others who had wisely chosen to move out West where they could establish a non-adjectival identity.

"Come on in, Big-John," said Lizzie as she swung the door wide. Usually during warm weather the door stayed open, but the baby's new mobility necessitated keeping it closed.

"Didn't know if you was home," Big-John said. "What with the door closed tight and no smoke comin' out the chimbley."

"The fire's banked low. No need for heat today. What do you mean—Rebecca's wool? In this bag?" she asked when she noticed the plump shorts-sack he carried under his arm.

"It's rent for Rebecca's sheep…" he started to explain as Rebecca leaned from the second-story window.

"That's all right, Lizzie," she called down. "I'll take care of it. I'll be right there, Big-John."

"Most times, I bring Rebecca her wool right after shearin'," he continued, "But this year, what with one thing and another, I be a trifle late."

"Yes," Lizzie said, "I heard Sunday that Hazel has been ailing. How is she?"

"Comin' along. Slow."

Rebecca quickly descended the back stairway, greeted Big-John and took his bag of wool.

"I weighed it 'fore I left home," he said.

"That's fine. It hefts about right. I'll take your word for it. How did the lambing go this spring?"

"Eight of 'em. Two dams had twins."

"Wasn't that fine?"

"Damn nuisance. Both of 'em nursed only one lamb. Now I got a couple o' cossets to feed. Damn nuisance."

"Why don't you keep both of them for a flock of your own."

"What you askin' for 'em? I can't 'ford much."

"Look here, Big-John. You've done fine taking care of my sheep and you always pay on time. Why don't you just take the two cossets as a bonus?"

"You're a good woman, Rebecca Gould."

Thus Lizzie learned something new about her remarkable mother-in-law. Since her marriage, she had frequently watched Rebecca use wool for trading, especially with the peddlers who came by regularly and who frequently left the dooryard complaining that they were hornswoggled by the old woman's sharp bartering. Rebecca also traded wool for worn clothes and blankets with the housewives of Lisbon and surrounding towns. These she tore into strips and wove into colorful rag rugs on her loom.

The same Indian lore that she practiced to extract medicines from herbs, bark and berries, enabled her to produce dyes to change dull clothing into the bright and cheerful floor coverings that neighbors vied to purchase. There were few homes or offices in the area that had not bought at least one of Rebecca's carpets to decorate an entryway or warm a bedroom floor.

Lizzie had wondered where the wool came from that Rebecca stored in heaps in the open chamber, for there seemed to be much more than could have been shorn from Tom's small flock.

After Big-John had gone, Rebecca disclosed that several local farmers rented sheep from her, paying annually for the privilege with a percentage of the wool. Whenever she accumulated more than she could store, she explained, she sold a few bags to the Worumbo Woolen Mills at the Falls.

A couple hours later, from the kitchen window Lizzie watched in silence as Tom drove Fan back to the stable. She hesitated to mention to the other two women her fear that Tom was having another attack, but she could think of no other reason why he would quit work so early in the day. Perhaps the heat was too much for him. It had been well over a month since his last spell and lately he seemed especially vigorous. Color had returned to his face replacing the jaundiced pallor of his illness.

In a few minutes, to her relief, he walked jauntily toward the back door. When he saw her in the window he waved a cigar box he was holding in his hand and motioned for her to join him in the yard.

"Time for a picnic," he exclaimed as she came out. "What d'you say, Lizzie? Let's make a bee festival up in the woods?"

"Gracious, Tom Gould, what's got into you?"

"You've been cooped up too long. Time to get out. Let's walk up to the pasture and find a bee tree."

"Don't be ridiculous. I've got too much work to do."

"It'll wait." He put his arm about her and propelled her away from the doorway.

"But we'll have to eat first."

"No time. We'll take a basket with us. All we need is bread and butter and some pickles. We'll pick berries. Lots o' berries comin' in."

"What about Ralph?"

"The women'll take care of him. Let's go."

"I don't know what to say."

"Don't say nothing. Got to hurry if we're goin' to get to the woods before eatin' time."

In a few minutes they were heading toward the pasture, Lizzie carrying the lunch basket and holding Tom's arm. Eunice had said, "Well, I declare!" and Ralph in his grandmother's arms was glumly watching his mother depart.

"Got to thinkin' about how cool the shade in the grove would be," Tom explained as they strolled along, "And then I remembered the swarm o' bees that got away last May, while I was laid up. I figured if we could find 'em, it wouldn't be a wasted afternoon."

"How in the world do you expect to locate a swarm of bees?"

"That's what this cigar box is for. I'll show you."

"Now, where did you ever find a cigar box?"

"In the shed. Probably belonged to Father. Guess he must of used it to locate the bees we got down in the orchard."

They followed the cow lane to the top of the hill, where he helped Lizzie over the stone wall. Then they cut across the meadow toward the oak and maple grove. He paused by a bed of white clover near the brook close to the edge of the woods.

"Here's a good spot," he said. He opened the box and showed Lizzie the block of honeycomb inside. "When they find this here honey, they'll think they're in bee paradise." He placed the box near the clover, leaving the cover open. "Now let's eat."

Lizzie's basket held a loaf of bread, some cheese, a pot of jam and two doughnuts and a pickle, the metal cup Tom had carried during the War and a mug for herself, all wrapped in a length of white toweling. While she spread the towel on a flat stump and set out the food, he brought water from the brook and cut several slices of bread.

"Now this here is a real bee festival," he said as he put his arm around her waist and suddenly kissed her cheek. He pointed to a moss-covered log nearby under the maples. "Won't you share my throne with me, my beautiful queen?"

"Why, Tom Gould, how you carry on. I've never seen you like this. What has got into you?"

"Ain't that the way they talk in those books you read."

"Now, maybe it is," she replied coyly. "Maybe it is. At any rate, your majesty, I'll be glad to join you."

While they were eating, he made several sorties to the cigar box, but finally shrugged with disgust.

"It's no use, Lizzie," he called. "Come over here. I'll show you what's happened. That's all right. The bees won't harm you when they're busy stealing my honey." She joined him in the field. There were ten or a dozen bees crawling over the honeycomb, with others arriving and departing in quick succession.

"You see that line of bees. They're all mine. Just watch this bee climbin' up the side of the box. (He pointed, almost touching the bee with his finger) See. He's heavy with honey. It's all he can do to fly...There he goes...Watch him circle...There now, now he heads out." He laughed aloud. "Hi, did you see that? He almost run into his ol' sidekick comin' back for another load."

"Is that what they mean by a bee-line?" Lizzie asked.

"It sure be. But look at the direction they're flyin' in. They're all aimin' right for the orchard. They've come from my own hives."

"Look! That one there...the one that just flew away," she pointed excitedly. "He's not going in the same direction."

"Ayuh. That's right. But he's one of Jake's. See, there's another bee-line headin' straight for Jake's barn."

"How on earth did they find this honey so quickly?"

"Don't know. But they talk to each other somehow. One of their scouts flew up here to be a monitor in the clover, but soon as he found my box, he hightailed it back to the hive and spread word that there was a gold mine up here. Just like Californie, he musta said."

"Where are the bees from that bee tree you talked about? Why aren't they here?"

"I guess we ain't fur enough away from home. Do you feel like walkin' a bit further? There's more clover on the fur side of the next field. Might have better luck over there...There's stones over the brook, so's you won't get your feet wet...And there's even a haycock we can rest on while we're waitin'"

"This is so interesting. Let's do it."

Tom shook the box, with his bare fingers picked out the bees that failed to fly away, and closed the lid.

"Aren't you afraid they'll sting?"

"Dhow," he replied confidently. "Not while they're full o' honey."

The August sun had passed the zenith and was on its way down the western sky, but it still beat relentlessly on them as they crossed the open field. While he set his bee trap anew, she sought a shady spot behind the haycock. The deep shadow of a solitary elm was moving toward her and soon enveloped the site she chose. She loosened her shirtwaist to feel the slight, cooling breeze that had arisen. Tom pulled down several armfuls of hay to make a comfortable seat for her.

"What a wonderful day," she murmured as Tom settled beside her. "I'm so content."

He took her hand in his and placed his left arm behind her.

She leaned her head against his shoulder…

How satisfying it would be to report that Mary Emma, their eldest daughter, was born nine months later, but despite their enthusiastic endeavors on that blissful summer afternoon, she did not arrive, in fact, for a full year. Also, Tom failed to locate his bee-tree, for when he finally inspected his bee-trap he found most of the honeycomb had vanished. A line of bees stretched into the grove, proving the bee-tree's existence. Now he knew its direction, but it was too late in the day and there was too little honey left to triangulate its exact location.

Mary Emma Gould was born on August 22, 1872.

CHAPTER 18

"Exercise is the remaining point in bringing up healthy families. All children incline to activity, so much so that they are fully prepared by weariness for frequent rest. Such activity should never be resisted, but encouraged by every means, especially by dress and suitable space. A bit of playground out of doors is a treasure, where it can be had, and a load of sand is a delight to children of any age, since it can be played with and leave no stains on them or their clothing. Even a small quantity of sand for indoor play gives many hours of pleasure, if it is poured upon a square of oil cloth and each child allowed a pail and spoon with which to amuse themselves. I once knew a woman who made use of a small pailful of yellow cornmeal. This she would pour upon a carpet, knowing it would only brighten the colors when finally removed with a brush. There is no need to buy expensive toys for children, but those parents who can do so doubtless derive much pleasure from the practice. Among children of every class play is a wonderful educator." **Science of Feeding Babies etc.:** H. Elizabeth Gould. Rebman Company, NY. (1916) Pg 76.

"A penny for your thoughts, Eunice," Tom's mother said when she noticed that her elderly step-daughter had dropped her knitting into her lap and was staring out the window.

"Well, Rebecca, if you must know. I was just watching Tom over on the other hill, shocking the corn," Eunice responded.

"He's been working at it all day," Lizzie said. She was in the rocking chair near the stove with Mary Emma nestled against her breast, grateful for a quiet moment while three-year-old Ralph was asleep in his crib.

"I guess I was having sort of a day-dream," Eunice went on, "Thinking about the corn huskings we used to have when I was a child. As soon as we saw the corn up in shocks, we knew it wouldn't be long before Father would be sending word for the neighbors to come over for a husking bee. Oh, those were such good times."

"Weren't they, indeed?" Rebecca agreed. "Remember old Hod Adams and his fiddle. How he could play! Reels and ballads, he knew them all."

"Tom never told me about Father Gould's husking bees," Lizzie said. "Were you still holding them when Tom was a boy?"

"Tom wouldn't remember them," Rebecca said. "After Jacob and I were married, we only had husking bees here in our barn perhaps a couple of years. Maybe three. When young Jake started having them over to his place, Jacob lost interest."

"Before Mother passed on, Rebecca," Eunice said, "You used to come every year with your old folks."

"That's right. How I looked forward to the Gould's husking bees!"

"I'd say it looks as if Tom's got plenty of corn this year," Eunice said. "Maybe, if you'd ask him, Lizzie, he'd have one this fall."

"Oh, Tom would just think I was being empty-headed," Lizzie protested. "He'd rather have us shuck his corn and get it done the way he wants it. I don't believe he'd trust it to somebody else."

"Husking bee's quicker," Eunice snapped.

Lizzie laughed apologetically.

"I don't know that I wouldn't rather husk our corn all by myself than spend two days cooking for a throng of merrymakers."

"All you'd have to do is bake a couple pots of beans," Eunice declared with a shrug of annoyance.

"And bread and pies and cake, et cetera," Lizzie added, trying to smile tolerantly.

"Well, if you don't want to ask him, Lizzie," Eunice declared. "I'll suggest it to him myself."

"I think Tom would enjoy a husking," Rebecca agreed.

✿   ✿   ✿

November 17, 1872,

Dear Sister Emma:

Tom has decided to have a husking bee on the twenty-sixth of November instant. There will be a number of your good friends in attendance. If you can come, it will be an opportunity for you to renew Lisbon acquaintances and at the same time meet our darling little Mary Emma. She is so dainty and as good as gold. I must say, after Ralph, she is a pure joy. I know driving here will be a long trip for you, but you can stay overnight and go to church with Mother Gould and me on Sunday before you head back for New Gloucester.

The husking bee was Sister Eunice's idea. Surely not mine. She proposed it last week when she saw Tom out in the field shocking the corn. At first he seemed to have agreed with her suggestion, but meanwhile he was doing nothing about it. And I must say I was just as well pleased, because with my two babies I surely have no need for all that extra cooking and preparation.

I don't really know whether Tom would have gone ahead with plans for a bee (for he was certainly getting no encouragement from me) if his brother Levi had not unexpectedly returned from the Maritimes. As soon as Levi heard about it, he immediately started handing out invitations.

Levi's arrival was quite a surprise, although for some time Mother Gould has been saying that his letters sounded as if he were ready to come home. He's been in New Brunswick for a number of years learning the stone mason trade. He may stay on here at the farm and work occasionally with his half-brother Stephen, who has a masonry business at the Falls, but such employment would not be steady. He has mentioned going to Boston to look for a permanent job and even talks about homesteading in the Dakotas with a friend of his. We shall see. He is certainly a different man than his brother Tom.

Besides the husking bee and the sudden return of Rebecca's "prodigal son", there is no real news here on the Ridge. Brother Caleb recently sent me "The Mill on the Floss" by the British writer George Eliot. I have been told that "George Eliot" is actually a fictitious name taken by a woman. I can believe it, for the story is told with great compassion and a deep religious conviction, reminding me of Harriet Beecher Stowe. Sister Eunice is reading the book now. Her eyes are not good and she reads very slowly, but as soon as she is finished (or gives up entirely) I will send it on to you, as Caleb instructed.

Have you heard that Susan B. Anthony was arrested on Election Day for attempting to vote? The poor woman! "The Enterprise", our local weekly, made no mention of the episode (although it had a long article on Gen. Grant's re-election), so perhaps you are not yet aware of it. "The Kennebec Journal", which finds its way into my hands occasionally, printed the whole story, although in a derisive manner, referring to Mrs. Anthony as a "female suffragist." It is difficult not to admire her courage, (as I am sure you do) even though one may not fully condone her vulgar behavior. You will surely join me in praying for her good fortune.

We have had several frosts and are now enjoying a number of days of Indian Summer. The frosts were severe enough to kill off the flies, for which I am grateful. It is so very difficult to keep them off the babies, as you most certainly know.

Your loving sister,
Elizabeth

❧   ❧   ❧

Many, many years later (1950) in his memoir ("Yankee Boyhood" R. E Gould, W. W. Norton & Co. Inc., NY) the fractious baby portrayed above would describe the husking bees as he remembered them:

"Sometimes when the corn was all in the barn, the ears broken off and piled on one side of the barn floor, the neighbors would be invited in for a husking bee. Father did not think much of this method because the young people who came to a husking bee were concerned with getting the husking over so that the games could begin, and the corn was not assorted in the careful manner he approved. Husks would be left on soft corn that was unfit for tracing, and seed corn would be thrown in with the regular corn and was apt not to dry as it should.

"However, we had an occasional husking. The corn was made ready and the invitations sent out. Nothing formal, just the word was passed to a few neighbors and they were asked to tell others. On the night of the husking they would begin to arrive from all quarters. Many would come for several miles. There would be a lot of strange faces and the girls would ask in hushed tones, 'Who is that fellow with the curly hair that came with the Potter boys'? Mother had been at work since daylight baking beans and making pies and cakes and puddings and all sorts of things. Baked beans were a standby for events of this sort. They usually had two and sometimes three kinds, such as Yellow Eye, Pea, and Red Kidney.

"The corn was husked in a short time, and, since the finding of a red ear gave the finder the privilege of kissing all the girls, some unprincipled young men were accused of carrying a red ear in their pockets. If my memory fails me not, no girl was enraged beyond her capacity for anger by these actions."

❦   ❦   ❦

Grace, second daughter and third child of Tom and Lizzie, was born on the twenty-eighth of June, 1874. The evening of Grace's arrival, the atmosphere was tense in the Gould kitchen. Levi had the Kennebec Journal open on the table before him, but he was not reading it. He fingered his walrus moustache as he stared out the window at the gathering twilight. Occasionally, he glanced with hostility at Tom, who was napping in the rocking chair across the room. Lizzie occupied the bed in Rebecca's room off the kitchen where the birth had taken place, the newborn asleep in a crib beside her. Rebecca had tucked the two older children into their beds on the second floor and was climbing wearily to a straw-filled mattress in the attic. Now sixty-three, she was exhausted by the summer heat and the frenzy of another birth. Eunice said she was worn out, but when no one responded she grabbed her cane and moved slowly toward her room.

Tom had spent the day working in the lower meadow with Fan, the mare. Levi weeded the vegetable garden back of the barn. Several times the women had called on him to watch the children or to bring something needed in the birthing room. By the end of the day, his resentment toward his brother was immense, but it grew even greater when Tom stopped by the garden patch in the late afternoon.

"You got to turn that pussley upside down or it'll just take root again," Tom had said as he surveyed the pile of weeds that Levi had pulled. For Tom to leave the house when his wife was having a baby was cause enough for Levi's anger, but to criticize his weeding was unforgivable, especially when Levi had been told by the same father, as many times as Tom had, to beware the tenacity of pussley.

As Rebecca stretched out on the pallet trying to institute comfort in her aching bones, she heard Levi coming up the stairs.

"Can I talk with you, Mother?" he called quietly. She pulled a blanket up over her nightclothes.

"I'm headin' out," he declared. After a pause, she groaned. Tears filled her eyes.

"I knew it," she said mournfully. "Just from your look I knew you'd been bickerin' with your brother again."

"That ain't it. It ain't just that me and Tom fight. The Good Book's full of brothers fighting each other. There's no way on God's earth I can work with him."

"Now, Levi, it's your farm just as much as it's his. Your father left us equal shares in it: you, me and Tom."

"I know that, but does Tom? I'll sell him my share cheap, just so's I don't have to work with him. I got to get out of here."

She reached out for her son's hand and pulled him towards her.

"Don't leave me, Levi. Please. I need you here. Stay home. Without you I wouldn't feel as if the place belonged to me. This is Lizzie's home now. It ain't mine. She's makin' changes every day."

For a long time he sat on the edge of his mother's bed holding her in his arms, while she wept. Finally he said:

"I'll tell you what. I'll stay until we find some place for you to go. Charlie Baker told me he was looking for someone to stay with Hattie. Maybe he'll make a home for you. You got your sheep money. Don't worry, Mother, I won't leave until you're taken care of."

CHAPTER 19

"None of us know why sin is in the world, but we have all observed that an honest fight with it builds healthy character." **Science of Feeding Babies etc.**: *H. Elizabeth Gould. Reb man Co. NY (1916) Pg. 47*

A week after Tom and Lizzie's wedding, her younger brother, Avery, had entered Bowdoin College in Brunswick, Maine. In the subsequent six years their paths had crossed only once when during a school holiday Avery had driven his parents to Lisbon to see their new grandson, Ralph. But there had been an occasional correspondence (Lizzie writing nearly three letters to each of Avery's replies). Now he was graduating.

August 11, 1875

Dearest Brother Avery,

Or should I now begin my letter to you in a more dignified fashion? Such as: My dear Dr. Avery Foster, M.D.

Father recently wrote that you have completed your studies the head of your class at the Medical School of Me. at Bowdoin. My affectionate congratulations. Do let me know promptly where you decide to practice. From the tone of his letter I can certify to you that your father is bursting his waistcoat buttons with pride over your triumph, although, of course, he may never admit to it—pride, even in a son's accomplishment, being a vice he totally repudiates.

As I have told you many times, I am so gratified that you chose medicine as your career. It would have been my own choice, had such a course been available. I still attempt to learn all I can about medicine, because the more a mother knows on the subject, the better she can care for her children.

I am very fortunate that all three of my children are robust, although tiny Grace is fussy and is not gaining weight as fast as I would like. She is just over a year old and I sometimes wonder if my milk totally agrees with her. Although it may seem improper to some, especially Father, for me to consult with a younger brother on this subject, I must. In view of your training I can see nothing wrong with such a discussion and I hope you agree. Tom's mother, who knows a great deal about babies, assures me that Grace is doing fine, but I keep hoping to discover a nutritious supplement to feed her if she does not pick up. Are unbolted whole wheat crackers softened in milk, as suggested by the late Mr. Graham, a sound choice? Have your studies informed you how soon bolstering diets can safely be fed to an infant? Write at once, if you have any information.

Tonight is the first opportunity I have had to write you since I was told of your graduation. I regret the delay. I find little time to do the things that mean so much to me, as writing to my family. I am home alone with the babies and they now are all securely asleep. Tom is at a meeting and may not be home for an hour or more. Gen. Neal Dow is lecturing at the GAR Hall. I had hoped to attend and was especially looking forward to his speech, for I have heard he is a stirring orator.

This morning, however, Mother Gould was summoned to care for a young woman whose time was not anticipated for several weeks. Sister Eunice, whom you met when you were here, retires to her room every evening after supper and cannot hear the babies when they cry. She is such a sweet woman that I cannot speak anything but praise for her, but I must say she continually undermines my discipline. I have only to speak sharply to Ralph and he runs weeping to his Aunt Eunice to receive a piece of toffee, a supply of which she always carries in her apron pocket. When I spank, she cuddles. But this is not your concern. I am only explaining why Tom went alone to the meeting.

Tom's brother Levi is also out again this evening, although I would not have left the children with him, either. You did not meet him for he had not yet returned from New Brunswick when you were here. He keeps saying that he wants to find work in Boston, but his mother discourages him from leaving.

Levi is a jolly fellow and I am sure you would like him, but I am uncertain whether he is the best influence for my children.

Gen. Dow's labors in spreading the gospel of temperance has been so worthwhile. I remember our discussion on the plague of rum (that time you visited us), as well as the firm position you have taken in your letters, so I am confident you agree with what I am saying. The nation needs men like Gen. Dow in the government, but I suppose so long as only men vote, less responsible persons than he will gain the power. Although the sale of alcoholic beverages has been forbidden in Maine for at least 20 years, I am afraid there are still members of the G.A.R. who need to hear Gen. Dow's message.

Tom never imbibes, for which I am grateful. As soon as the cider begins to turn in the barrel, he adds mother of vinegar to avoid tempting the hired hands. I suspect that his brother Levi still must learn that there is no nutrition in ardent spirits. However, I also suspect that this evening he is avoiding the General's exemplary discourse.

If you get a chance before you settle permanently in your own promised land, come to Lisbon to see me and my handsome family. If you cannot arrange such a trip, know that you are taking with you my deepest affection and our fervent desire that you find nothing but success and happiness in your future. May the good Lord guide your steps.

Your devoted sister Elizabeth

A group of veterans and their wives were gathered at the entrance of the GAR Memorial Hall awaiting the arrival of the guest of honor, Gen. Neal Dow, who, they had learned from the Post Adjutant, was dining with Judge Jack in his great mansion overlooking the Androscoggin Valley. A farm wagon was approaching along Sabattus Pike. As it neared, Lil Farrar said:

"That looks like Tom Gould—all alone. I thought you said Lizzie was coming with him."

"That's what she told me the other day," her husband replied. "Said she wouldn't miss hearing General Dow. Said she'd be here by hook or by crook."

"Hope she's not sick." She moved down the steps toward the rail where Tom would be hitching Fan. "Where's Lizzie?"

"She couldn't make it, Lil. Stayed home with the babies."

"She's not sick?"

"Dhow, she's fine." He swung himself out of the seat and jumped to the ground. "Greetings and salutations, men," he called toward the crowd, waving his hand over his head. "Hain't the General here yet?"

In a few minutes, a carriage arrived with the General and Mrs. Jack facing the Judge, whose back was toward the driver.

"Let's go on in," Lil said to Tom. "The Hall's filling up. Mother Farrar's been saving four seats for us up front, but without Lizzie we'll need only three."

"You two go ahead," said Tom. "Don't save me a seat. If I go in, I'll stand in back."

"Ain't you goin' in?" Frank asked.

"After, maybe. Thought I might stay out here an' chew the rag for a while."

The General and the Jacks descended from their carriage, stopped briefly on the steps to allow the Judge to introduce Dow to the G.A.R. leaders, and then swept into the auditorium, followed by all but five stragglers. Horace Jordan, who stood beside Tom, exploded:

"By-god-you-mister, ain't he the bantam rooster?" One-Eyed John Coombs chuckled at the comment, nodding enthusiastically. The rest moved over toward the railing and sat down on the steps.

"Ain't you goin' inside?" Tom asked Jordan.

"Not if I can help it, by-god-you-mister. I don't let nobody preach at me on Sunday mornin's, why put up with it, I say, b'god, on a Tuesday night?"

"General Dow ain't a preacher, be he?" One-Eyed John asked. The other four laughed.

"If rum's the devil, he be," Jack Winslow answered. "I get enough preachin' on that text from the Woman."

"Amen," said Tom.

"What're you 'amenin' about, Tom?" asked Horace. "You wouldn't take a drink, b'god, if you was drownedin' in it."

"I was talkin' 'bout the preachin'."

Tom's third daughter and fourth child, Louise Hinkley Gould, was born to Lizzie, May 3, 1876. Dr McLellan attended.

During the preceding February there had been a break in the weather and on the 24th Tom harnessed Fan to the sleigh for a trip into town for supplies. Lizzie appeared unexpectedly in the stable doorway dressed in a hat and a shabby woolen coat.

"I believe I'll ride in with you," she said.

"You think that's a good idea? You're gettin' pretty big."

"If I can pitch hay to a cow, I trust it will be safe for me to ride into the village."

"What're you goin' to do when you get there?"

"Some errands."

"Tell 'em to me. I'll do 'em for you."

"I don't believe you can."

"Why not?"

"Isn't it enough that I ask to ride with you? I shouldn't have to answer questions. I've been cooped up all winter and Mother Gould says she will watch out for the children. It's so seldom she's here with us these days."

"It's no wonder," Tom grumbled. "She says you never let her do anything."

"Oh, Tom. Let's not quarrel again. Your mother is just as good as she can be, but there just is no room for two women running this house. And Mother Gould is more energetic than most women half her age. We get in each other's way and on each other's nerves. I'm delighted she has something worthwhile to do and just visits with us. I'm sure we're both happier."

"She still owns a third of the estate."

"Please, Tom, leave it to your mother and me to work it out."

With obvious reluctance, Tom finished harnessing Fan. He moved a box he had placed on the seat to make room for Lizzie and silently they headed down the hill toward the village.

Returning home later in the day, Tom asked:

"What did you come for? You ain't got no packages."

"I went to see Dr. McLellan."

Tom, who was slouched in his seat, straightened abruptly. He started several times to speak before he was able to sputter:

"Now you look a-here, Lizzie. I ain't got no money to pay some damned quack that nobody needs. Your health's good. You ain't had a doctor for any of the three you've gotten already."

"Tom, I want a doctor."

"Want's no damn reason for spendin' money we ain't got."

"I'm sure we can afford to pay for a doctor."

"Mother takes care of you good."

"Yes, she did."

"Well, by God, she'll do it again."

"No, Tom, this baby is going to have a doctor. I've talked it over with Mother Gould and she agrees with me. Dr. McLellan will come when I send for him."

Tom was aghast. He could only stammer.

"If you won't fetch Dr. McLellan when my time comes," Lizzie continued after a moment, "Jake says he will."

"Damn you, Lizzie."

She raised her chin and looked straight ahead. She made no reply.

CHAPTER 20

"Consecrated bodies, clean thoughts, and peaceful minds have much to do with the perfect fulfilling of any function. The hopeful, happy mother has everything in her favor; while the forces of nature are much depressed by a worrying, self-pitying spirit." **Science of Feeding Babies etc."** *H. Elizabeth Gould. Rebman Co. N.Y. (1916) Pg. 85*

September, 1877, Mary Emma entered the first grade of the one-room schoolhouse at the four-corners up the hill. By this time Ralph was, chronologically, in the third grade but for most subjects, since he was the only member of his class, he studied with the four girls in the grade ahead of him. All too frequently, both classes were merged with the three dull fifth-grade boys. Whenever the teacher could combine classes she never hesitated and Ralph responded to the challenge. The older boys resented being outshone by a mere baby and spent much of their time devising stratagems to humiliate him.

Even at the age of eight Ralph already had a variety of home chores, either before or after school: carry the swill that had accumulated in the kitchen to the pig pen; feed the poultry; pick up the eggs; split kindling; fill the wood boxes in the kitchen and in Aunt Eunice's room (also Grandmother's room on the rare occasions now when she was home); and, until the snows came and closed down the meadows, drive the milch cows to the pasture mornings and bring them home evenings.

In addition, as a preventative of mischief, Tom frequently gave his son additional tasks, such as weeding or piling up the stones that the frost heaved every winter to the surface of the garden. Occasionally, when Tom's chronic infirmities came upon him suddenly, he would retire to his bedroom to rest and leave his son with instructions to stop working only when his job was finished. Later, watching from the second floor, Tom might become angry and shout at Ralph out the bedroom window to stop dallying.

Lizzie did not interfere. Man's work was Tom's calling. Only once did she summon the temerity to suggest that perhaps this was a strenuous schedule for a small boy going to school. Tom responded bluntly that work had not hurt him and it was never too early for a boy to learn. Lizzie concluded that she should leave character building to her husband and devote her attention only to the nutritional and spiritual aspects of rearing her family.

Evenings after supper she sat in her rocking chair with the baby Louise in the cradle beside her, holding Grace in her arms, with Mary and Ralph kneeling on either side while she read aloud to them inspirational poetry or passages from the Bible. Afterward, the two older children with tightly closed eyes and bowed heads would recite the prayer their Aunt Jennie had written some years before her death:

> *With every evening, may I be*
> *Nearer, blest home, to God and thee*
> *And may each trial teach my soul*
> *One lesson more of self control.*
> *Each drop of dew, each sunbeam's ray,*
> *Is needed to perfect the day;*
> *Darkness and sunlight must combine*
> *To work their mission all divine:*
> God bless Father and Mother;
> God bless Grandmother and Aunt Eunice;
> God bless Uncle Levi
> God bless Grace and Louise;
> God bless Mary Emma {Ralph} and myself;
> God bless everybody. Amen.

Several months earlier (actually before the birth of Louise) Ralph had asked his mother why Uncle Jake and Aunt Aphia were left out of the prayer. Since this seemed a reasonable suggestion those two names were subsequently inserted after Uncle Levi. Emboldened by success, Ralph continued as time went on to propose other persons in need of benediction. The list grew, until his mother caught on toward the end of the school year—when he insisted on including the names of the three hostile fifth-grade boys—that the expanded recitation was more a bedtime delaying tactic than a concern for anyone's salvation. The litany was again reduced to embrace only those who lived under the same roof with the children.

When Lizzie told the family of Ralph's amusing ruse, Eunice applauded the intelligence of her nephew; Rebecca, home for a few days, expressed surprise that it had taken her grandson's mother so long to penetrate his deception. Tom said he wasn't aware that Ralph had been having trouble with the boys at school.

"I'll work closer with him," said Tom, "And get to know him better."

"That'll be good," said Lizzie.

🍁   🍁   🍁

"You come from a family of soldiers," Tom told Ralph a few days later while Tom was hoeing and Ralph was picking up stones. Ralph stood erect to think about this unexpected bulletin.

"Uncle Levi wasn't a soldier, was he?" he asked skeptically.

This was not the direction Tom had planned the conversation to take. He mulled several answers before he said:

"Well, no. I volunteered. Your uncle had to stay here on the farm to help your grandfather. But I was the soldier" he straightened his shoulders, "...in the Union Army."

"Was Uncle Jake a soldier?"

"No."

"Was my grandfather a soldier?"

"Not exactly," and he added hurriedly, "But his father was. And your great, great granddad (That's your grandfather's grandfather) he was killed on the Plains of Abraham during the Siege of Qweebec." He paused to let Ralph think about the importance of the message. "That was durin' the French and Indian Wars. Have they learnt you yet about the French and Indian Wars?"

"I think so."

"Your great grandfather, Joseph, he went to war along with his father; they trudged all the way to Canady with General Wolfe. Do you know where Canady is?"

Ralph nodded hesitantly.

"They was at the Siege of Qweebec. Your great grandfather was a mess boy. He was only thirteen years old but he volunteered the same day his father did."

"Is a mess boy a soldier?"

"Not exactly, but he fights with soldiers. He carries food, helps get meals, that sort o' thing."

"I'll bet he carried a musket?"

"I'll say he did. After his father died he had to carry his big, heavy gun all the way back home. The "Queen's Arm" they called it, or so your grandfather told me."

"What's a siege?"

Tom had intended this chat to be about his own military adventures, not a history lesson, but he was obligated to go on.

"Well," he began, "It's when there's a city and an army surrounds it…The army tries to keep provisions from goin' in and out…For God sake, Ralph, don't they learn you in school what a siege is?"

"I don't know. Maybe. We learnt about the Revolution. Did they have a siege in the Revolution?"

"How should I know? I ain't a teacher."

"Did Grandfather fight in the Revolution?"

"He wasn't old enough. He was just a boy."

"Why wasn't he a mess boy?"

"He was only six years old."

"I guess Lucien Fortin's old enough to be a mess boy."

"Who in tarnation's Lucy Fortin?"

"His name ain't Lucy. It's Lucien. He's a Pea Eye. He's one of the boys in school. He's almost fourteen. Would they let Pea Eyes be mess boys?" Tom stopped hoeing and said with some surprise:

"I didn't know you had Pea Eyes in your school. I thought them critters went to the Pope's school down to the Falls along with the Bohunks," adding while Ralph was thinking about this information, "If they ever go to school at all."

"Lucien's a great, big feller," Ralph explained, stretching his hand above his head in demonstration. Tom was obviously not interested in Lucien's size.

"I guess that'd be about right," he mused aloud, but mostly to himself. "I remember now. One o' the Davis girls did get hitched to a Canuck from down to Frogtown. They're livin' up back o' the Davis place. I guess his name might o' been Fortin."

"What's it mean, a Pea Eye?" Ralph asked.

"You better not let your mother hear you callin' anybody a Pea Eye."

"That's what the boys call Lucien in school."

"That may be. But when you're around your mother, you'd better call him a Frenchman. Or a Canadian. Is he one of the boys that's been pickin' on you?"

Ralph nodded.

"I figured," said Tom as he laid his hoe down and sat on a nearby boulder. "Pea Eyes don't know much. Just watch he don't steal from you…Why don't we stop work for a couple o' minutes? And I'll sit here on this rock. I'll tell you a bit about the soldierin' I've done."

Ralph, welcoming the break, straddled the root of a gnarled apple tree and leaned against the trunk.

"Did I ever tell you about me bein' took prisoner?"

Ralph suppressed an affirmative response. It was one of his father's favorite stories, but for the sake of "a pause in the day's occupation" (A phrase from one of his mother's favorite verses) he was willing to hear it again.

"Well, I was lucky," Tom began. He described in grim detail the battlefield at Gettysburg and the dreadful bloodshed of the first day of fighting. He had fired his muzzle-loader at the enemy and had ducked behind a remnant of a shed, still standing after hours of shelling, to wait for his gun barrel to cool enough to reload. There he surprised three rebel soldiers who were lying low for the same purpose. He ordered them to surrender, but they outnumbered him and he was marched off behind the enemy lines a captive.

For the next two days he was moved from site to site, as the battle lines ebbed and flowed, at no time moving so far that he couldn't still hear the gun fire. He had no idea how the fighting was going until on the fourth day things quieted down and they started heading south. Then he knew the Rebels were retreating. Finally they stopped. Nobody said where. For a couple of weeks or more, maybe longer, they kept him under guard in a bivouac with a group of other prisoners.

One morning they were lined up and marched down a road and out into the country.

"I guess I was the only whole one in the batch. The rest had their heads banged up or their arms bandaged, or were walkin' on crutches. I'd been lucky.

We walked for hours. Some o' the men said we was goin' to be shot, some said they was goin' to put us on a steam train and ship us down to Georgia, and some said we was to be swapped for some Johnny Rebs. And that's what happened."

It took him another week or ten days, he continued, to get back to the 16th Maine. They had listed him as missing and didn't know what had happened to him. But he was welcomed back just the same. Then, he discovered how lucky he had been to be taken captive, because most of his mates had been killed or wounded during the two days of battle following his disappearance.

Ralph had been sitting quietly during the long narrative and he didn't want it to stop. Now, his father was gazing across the valley as if the battlefield were spread before him, but Ralph knew that unless he took action they would soon be back at work.

"Was that when you went swimmin'?" Ralph asked, certain that his question would spawn another story.

Tom laughed reminiscently.

"You remember that one? Aye yes," he agreed, "That was the time I went swimmim." He chuckled and started a new tale. "It was hot, hotter than Tophet. There's no place on earth hotter than Maryland in July and that's where we was. The Rebs couldn't spare more than a few men to watch over the whole parcel of us prisoners, so when we run out o' drinkin' water they didn't have nobody to send for some more. So they picked out a half dozen o' us Yankees who could still walk and give us each a couple o' buckets and set two guards to march us down to a river about a mile away. We had to climb down a steep bank to get to the water and by the time we got there we was all sweatin' like horses, the guards, too. Somebody said—I think it was Perkins who hailed from down Wiscasset way—that the water looked mighty temptin'. Anyways, he was the one who fell in."

Ralph laughed hilariously for he'd heard the story before and knew what was coming.

Tom described how Perkins pled with the guards for permission to take his duds off and wring them out, all the time standing in the water up to his neck. First the guards said no, but then they gave the go-ahead and Perkins began to undress. Another prisoner fell into the stream. Then another.

Tom described how the guards conferred and then gave permission for the whole party to strip and jump in. As the Yanks cavorted and splashed each other they kept calling to the Rebs, who were standing on the bank with their guns at the ready, to join them.

"Will you promise not to escape?" a guard demanded.

"Absolutely," Perkins yelled back.

"Everybody promise?"

"Sure," the Yanks agreed.

"Raise your hands and swear."

Each naked Yankee thrust his hands into the air, some treading water in the deep part of the stream.

"We swear," they cried.

"On your Christian honor?"

"On our Christian honor," they all yelled.

With that assurance the perspiring guards stacked their guns against a tree, shed their uniforms, and joined the swimmers. For fifteen long minutes the young men of two armies sported together in the refreshing waters of a nameless creek, forgetting the enmity that had been separating them.

Suddenly there was an explosion and a cannonball flew high over the stream and shattered a tree that stood on the opposite hill. Another. Then there were gunshots and a spent bullet splashed nearby. So intent had the soldiers been on enjoying a cooling swim, no one had noticed the armies approaching from both directions. By the time they had dressed and were skirting the edge of the river to find a safe route back to the prison encampment, a battle was raging overhead.

"Why didn't you run away?" Ralph asked.

"I give my pledge, and a soldier don't go back on his pledge."

"What's a pledge?"

"A pledge is…Well, anyways, I didn't have an idea what side o' the river the Union Army was on."

On the eighth of October, 1878, a few months after the above discussion with his first son, Tom's second son was born, Franklin Farrar, named for his friend and fellow veteran. Dr. McLellan was again in attendance, fortunately.

Franklin was born with six fingers on each hand. His right hand had a perfectly formed, workable second little finger, but on his left the extra finger was only rudimentary, a limp length of cartilage hanging from the edge of his hand. The doctor snipped it off with sheep shears that Ralph brought in from the shed. He bandaged the little fist, and promised to be back in a few days with instruments to remove the other superfluous digit.

❦ ❦ ❦

In her next letter to her brother Howard and his wife Sarah Lizzie made no mention of Franklin's affliction.

November 15, 1878

Dear Howard and Sarah:

It was thoughtful of you to send a beautiful flag in honor of Franklin's birth. How the country grows! Just imagine!—our nation with 38 states, our flag with 38 stars. Tom is also appreciative and tells me to add his thanks to mine. It will be flown at our door on all patriotic occasions.

I also agree with you that Franklin is a splendid name, but I am not sure that Tom does. Although our baby is named for his friend, Mr. Farrar, who volunteered on the same day and served with him during much of the War, it was touch and go for a while whether the name would be Franklin. As soon as Tom learned I was quick with child, he announced that if it were a son he would be named for the great Peter Cooper. Although I admire Mr. Cooper, I was less than enthusiastic about his running for President. I try not to spend much time on political questions, but it certainly seemed to me that the Independent Party and their Mr. Cooper totally ignored the needs of mothers and children, even more than that Democrat Mr. Tilden. Printing paper money might help the farmer, but it offers no solution to our nation's other problems. President Hayes is an admirable man, who seems dedicated to binding up the remaining wounds of the dreadful war. If women could have voted, and I know Sarah agrees, his victory would have been decisive. I believe in the end Tom voted Republican. He cast his first vote for A. Lincoln and has been a Republican ever since. (I am surmising, for Tom never discusses anything of a political nature with me)

Although I greatly admire Mr. Cooper's philanthropies, I certainly had no intention of allowing a son of mine to be named for anyone so narrow-minded. I should not be divulging this stratagem to you, except from your letters I know that you both agree with me. I told Tom that I had hoped that if we had a son he might be named after our good friend and should we have a daughter she could be named Lillian for Mrs. Farrar. Tom nodded and said he would think about it.

The next time I saw Lil Farrar, I told her that Tom was thinking of naming our child after Frank, if it turned out to be a boy, and, of course, she immediately told her husband, which was exactly what I had hoped and expected. Within a few days, Frank had told Tom that he was flattered. When my sweet baby was born, the dreadful name Peter Cooper was forgotten, for Tom now had no choice. Unless we named our son Franklin Farrar, his closest friend would feel slighted. Do you think I behaved terribly to do such a thing?

Again, I thank you, Brother, and dear Sarah for your thoughtful gift.

With very best wishes,
Elizabeth.

CHAPTER 21

"There is danger for us on every side, if we misinterpret signals. Pain is a true friend, though generally treated as an enemy. Often to a young mother it seems perfectly needless that, as often happens, the gentle nursing of her new baby should causehard pains in the region of her uterus. The pain announces contractions, which are very useful just then. They indicate safe closing of activities in that department, that all the forces may concentrate upon the new scheme of lactation. **Science of Feeding Babies etc.:** *H. Elizabeth Gould. Rebman Company, NY. (1916) Pg. 139.*

January 1, 1880

Dearest Mother:

Just a note to let Father and you know that here on Lisbon Ridge we are well as we start the new year and a new decade. I have had no time to write a letter. Ralph brought the chicken-pox home from school and it went through the whole family except for baby Franklin. Dr. McLellan says that infants seem to have an immunity. How interesting! We are finally through that siege, although Grace still has a few spots on her chest where she scratched the scabs. Blessedly, Tom has not had one of his spells for several weeks so I was spared the heavy barn chores while the children were ill. We see little of Mother

Gould. Sister Eunice has been laid up again with a quinsy and is an extra care, but she stays close to her room. Ralph, when I prod him, has been good about supplying her with wood and keeping the fire going in her stove. Sister Aphia drops in, but she is getting so hard of hearing I don't find her easy to talk to. I have so little time to read. The last book Father sent sits on the shelf where I put it when it arrived. It has been weeks since I have even been to church services—truly since summer. I should not complain. God has been good—we have food to eat, a roof over our heads and, in spite of the chicken-pox, the children stay healthy. Do write me.

With true affection,
Elizabeth

For the three weeks after Lizzie wrote this note to her parents, there was snow almost every day; then a couple of days of thaw and drizzle. But on January 24th, the sun rose bright. During the night the temperature had dropped. When Jake Gould, Tom's elderly half-brother who lived on his own farm a half mile down the hill, looked out the frosted window of his bedroom he could see that the crust was ideal for sledding. He proclaimed to his wife Aphia that today was the day he was going in to town. It was obvious that the trip was as much to hear different voices as to get supplies.

"Why don't you drop me off to the home place when you go by?" Aphia proposed. "I hain't seen Lizzie since before Christmas."

The jaunt to the village had been pleasant for Jake, but while he was sojourning with his friends around the stove at the feed store a northeast wind had arisen, so penetrating that on the way home the drifting crystals drove straight through his clothes. He now yearned to raise his feet before his own fire. He turned his little mare into the dooryard of the big farmhouse, and found shelter from the wind. The steam from the horse and his own breath enveloped him.

"C'mon, Wife," he bellowed toward the door without moving from the sleigh. "Let's git movin'. My feet's afreezin'."

In a moment the front door opened a crack and Grace peered out.

"Mother says to come in and get warm, Uncle Jake," she called.

"Can't stop. Tell your aunt to git a wiggle on." There was a pause while Grace relayed the message and awaited instructions from within.

"She'll be right out," she said and, shivering, closed the door. Jake tucked his beard into his collar which he drew closer around his neck and over his ears. He hunched his shoulders and shoved his mittened hands back under the robe.

Straightaway, Aphia was at the door, still talking over her shoulder to the folks inside. A heavy winter coat was bundled around her and her bonnet was anchored to her coiled bun of hair with a long hat pin. The red prism dazzled in the sun. Ralph was by her side.

"Be careful, Wife, them steps look prodigious slippery." Jake's muffled voice came from under his wraps. "Help your aunt over the ice, Boy,"

"That's what I'm here for," said Ralph.

Cautiously, the old woman edged toward the sleigh, Ralph holding her left elbow while her right hand grasped at the gaunt, ice-covered branches of the lilac bush that grew beside the walk.

"Easy there, Wife, even if you can't hear me," Jake mumbled, his watery eyes watching through the slit between his collar and the edge of his knitted cap. Slowly she groped around the sleigh and Ralph boosted her into the seat beside her husband.

"Git along," Jake ordered, slapping the reins against his horse's back. It was only a short ride down the hill to their home. While Jake was unharnessing the mare in the stable and covering her with a blanket, Aphia opened the draft on the kitchen stove and added wood. By the time Jake came in, the room was beginning to be warm.

"Big-John Coombs was tellin' me Tom's under the weather again," he shouted to his deaf wife as he hung his coat on the hook by the shed door.

"Yes and in this cold, Lizzie has all those barn chores to do as well as take care of her family. Tom's still abed. Complains about everything. How did Big-John find out about Tom bein' down?"

"Guess Frank Farrar stopped by the Farm yesterday."

"Who'd you say? What kind o' farmer?"

"Farrar! Frank Farrar. Tom's friend."

"Oh, you saw Frank in town this mornin'?"

"No, but he was to town afore I got there an' told Big-John." He leaned his head over to shout directly into her ear. "They was talkin' about Tom when I come in."

"Well, they should be. And nothin' good, neither. I tell you, Jake, that brother of yours has got no need bein' so contrary, just because he's bilious. Three times whilst I was there he pounded on his bedroom floor with a piece o' cordwood. The whole house shook. You'd a thought the Injuns was trying to git in. Three times Lizzie sent Ralph up to find out what he wanted, and three times she finally had to go herself. He didn't want nothin'. You might o' known. Just bein' a pest. One time, he told her to tell the young'ns to hush, he was tryin' to sleep. I tell you, Jake, I don't know why Lizzie puts up with him."

"She ain't gut much choice. But as long as I gut one, I'm stayin' away. As long as Niah was around, it was one thing, but I gut better things to do with my time than take care o' Tom's livestock…What did Lizzie say, anyways?" he asked as he warmed his hands over the stove.

"She didn't say nothin'. Yessir, she's a reg'lar saint an' a martyr, I tell you. That mite of a woman—up afore daylight, milkin' cows, shovelin' out the tic-up, pitchin' down fodder, an' then housework an' all them young'ns. Never stops. She was churnin' butter when I gut there. Still with the old slop churn. You know right well Tom can afford to buy her a new one. But he won't. When your father was alive and runnin' the farm, his children didn't run around looking like raga brash. What's Tom do with his money, anyways? The farm always made a livin' when your father was alive. All them youngsters to care for an' Lizzie's gut nothin' but rags to put on them. Nothin' for her to wear neither. I'll bet you a pretty penny it's been five years since she had a new dress."

"What she need of a new dress? With them five young whippersnappers she ain't goin' no place. It still be only five, ain't it?"

"I'll tell you one thing, Jake Gould." Aphia was wound up. She neither heard nor had time to respond to her husband's ill-advised questions. "Tom just don't know how lucky he be. Why, Lizzie's better than three hired hands."

"Tom knows well enough…After Niah gut married, he soon learnt not to count on me," Jake added.

"I ain't suggestin' you git mixed up with him, Jake. I'm just thinkin' o' Lizzie.

"She's still gut Eunice. Eunice run the farm for years afore Lizzie ever showed up."

"Eunice!" Aphia exploded. "You hain't seen your sister since summer, have you?. The old quinsy's come back on her. Wheezin' and coughin'. She's more trouble than she's help. I told you she was sick the last time I see Lizzie—over a month ago. She's been abed ever since. Come down to the kitchen this mornin' just to see me. First time she's been outa her room in over a month, Lizzie said.

Your sister's a sick old woman, Jake. She can't even rock the baby the way she be."

"You never told me Eunice was that sick."

"That ain't all. Whilst I was there, Grace grabbed a spoon away from Louise and made her cry and Lizzie slapped her hand. You'd a done the same thing. Grace lets out a howl and off she goes bellyaching to her Aunt Eunice, who reaches in her apron and takes out a sweetie. That's all Grace was crying for: a sweetie from her Aunt Eunice. All that old woman is, I tell you, is just another complication for Lizzie."

"Eunice always spoilt the young'ns, I guess."

"Wouldn't do you no harm if you'd go up and sit with your sister sometime, even if you don't hanker after doin' your half-brother's chores for him."

"I ain't goin' today," he muttered under his breath but she heard him, nonetheless.

"I'll remind you when the weather moderates," she responded.

Jake started to reply as Aphia paused but thought better of it. She went on:

"I told Lizzie she ought to insist on Rebecca stayin' home an' helpin' her, but she just laughed kind o' sadlike and said: 'Mother Gould's got the freedom to be herself'."

"What'd she mean by that?"

"Don't rightly know. But Lizzie don't seem to be blamin' her mother-in-law for her predicament." Aphia shook her head slowly.

"Why, what's Rebecca up to these days, anyways?" Jake asked.

"Speak up. What d'you say?" She cupped her hand behind her ear.

"Rebecca. What she doin'?" he shouted.

"She's over to Charlie Baker's. Lizzie says Hattie's expectin' again. I don't know what Hattie needs help for. She's only got one young'n, but, if they'll have her over there, I can't fault Rebecca for movin' off the farm. She's got that money from her sheep. It ain't much, but up to Baker's she' gut no warrant to spend it on her grandchildren."

"Did Lizzie tell you that?"

"Not Lizzie. She don't say a word. But I can see. I got eyes. Rebecca knows what she's doin'. Tom ain't takin' care of his family the way he ought to, the way they should be taken care of if he had half a mind."

"What d'you expect me to do about it?"

She laughed sardonically.

"Just listen to me rant, I guess. Sometimes Lizzie runs with a high check rein and there's lots she says that goes right over my head, but she sure is a worker and she ain't gittin' no help from Tom. Maybe he was a good soldier, but he sure ain't much of a husband."

❧   ❧   ❧

However, a year later, 1881, on February 28th, Lillian Wallace Gould was born. Named for Frank Farrar's wife, she was Tom and Lizzie's sixth child and fourth daughter. The night was bitter cold, and Lillian arrived a few minutes before Dr. McLellan.

Tom had performed the delivery. Ralph had ridden Tantrabogus into the village to summon the doctor, but the snow and ice had slowed the trip back.

CHAPTER 22

The greatest need that a child has is to be loved by responsible people. Its food is next in importance, but the wealthiest parent can provide nothing better than cow's milk for his baby, and the poor man can surely provide that. Then the bread and plain varieties of food which the working man needs are better for the growing child than costly dainties. Clothing may be costly, but it need not be so. A mother must have an ideal and work for it if she would give her child a chance in the world. They must be clean and neatly dressed..." Science of Feeding Babies etc.: H. Elizabeth Gould. Rebman Co. NY. (1916) Pg. 52.

A swarm of bees in May
Is worth a load of Hay;
A swarm of bees in June
Is worth a Silver Spoon;
A swarm of bees in July—
Leave them to Fly.

—Bee keeper's rhyme

❦   ❦   ❦

"Who in Hell moved a beehive while I was gone?" Tom demanded as he entered the kitchen. He was returning from the G.A.R. Encampment, Decoration Day, 1881, at the Fair Grounds in the nearby town of Topsham. For all his sickness he was still fit and his anger gave him the ruddy complexion of a well man.

Lizzie looked up from the stove where she was stirring a pot of stew. She had been heading toward the window seat where baby Lillian was screaming for nourishment when she remembered the stew and stopped to keep it from burning on. Two-year-old Franklin had moved the ladder-back chair that she had placed to keep the baby from falling off the window seat and was now pushing it across the floor. Grace, aged seven, was angrily attempting to wrest the chair from her brother's grasp, as her mother had desperately instructed, while Louise, the four year old, was placidly watching her infant sister flail her arms near the edge of the seat despite cries from her mother to do something to prevent a catastrophe. Mary Emma, the eldest at nine, dashed from the sink, where she had been peeling potatoes, just in time to rescue Lillian before she rolled to the floor.

"You're home, Tom?" Lizzie observed wearily as she glanced toward him. He watched impatiently as she took the baby from Mary Emma, unfastened her shirtwaist, seated herself in the ancient rocking chair by the window and began to nurse. The rounded peg of the left rear leg slipped in and out of its rocker with a sharp snap each time she rolled back in the chair.

"Which beehive?" she asked finally.

"By God almighty, you know which one," Tom exploded. "There's only one been moved."

"Tom, there's no call for taking the Lord's name in vain."

"Drop that bunk. I want to know who moved that hive. Those bees are ready to swarm and you can't tell what'll happen when you go cartin' a hive around."

"I suspect Ralph brought out a fresh hive this morning," Lizzie said, looking calmly into space as she moved Lillian's head to fit more comfortably against her arm. "That's probably the one you're talking about."

"I'm talkin' about that hive that's asittin' over under the summer-sweet tree. Why the devil would Ralph bring out another hive? Where in hell is Ralph, anyways? Off sporting, I'll bet."

"Tom, not in front of the children. Be careful with your language."

"Answer my question, dammit."

"Tom," she said in exasperation. "We can't have this sort of talk in front of the children."

"Will you answer my question?" his voice rose in anger.

"I will discuss nothing so long as you are speaking improperly."

Enraged, he clenched his fists and strode toward his wife. The children became silent, glancing anxiously from their father to their mother. Tears of fright welled into Louise's eyes. She cried out, a piercing sob. As suddenly as his anger flared, Tom wheeled toward Louise, paused a moment and then fled through the door he had just entered.

"Mary Emma," Lizzie said after a moment. "Please give the stew a stir." She continued to nurse, but offered her other arm to Louise who ceased sobbing as she climbed into her mother's lap.

❋   ❋   ❋

May 31, 1881

Dearest Sister:

I hope you will forgive my choosing you, but I must recount to somebody the dreadful day I spent yesterday. Never mention this letter to Father nor to Mother. Yesterday morning Tom went off to one of his G.A.R. "encampments" and he was hardly out of sight when Ralph came running in to say that bees were swarming in the summer-sweet tree. There was nothing I could do about it. You know how bees sting me. Ralph, dear boy, asked if he could hive them and I said he could try. He has helped his father hive bees in the past.

Sometime later I heard him wail. When I looked out bees were after him and he was running toward the back door. He had stings on his hands and face and a few welts on his back where bees had gotten under his shirt. I removed the stingers while Grace brought mud from the pond and we poulticed him up in good shape. He didn't seem much the worse for his experience. In fact, he wanted to go back and try again, but suddenly we heard a great buzzing and the whole swarm flew by the kitchen window on its way to the woods.

The first thing Tom spotted when he got home was the beehive Ralph had set under the swarm. He thought we had moved a working hive. Apparently, this is a bad thing to do during swarming season. At any rate he was fit to be tied. I was shocked at the language he used and cautioned him that the children were present. Then he came toward me and I was fearful that he intended me harm. The children started to cry. As soon as he heard them, he turned on his heel and went outdoors.

Shortly afterwards Ralph came home. (He had been up to the schoolyard playing with friends.) I was so afraid that Tom would take out his anger on Ralph that I hurriedly fed the children and shooed them all off to bed. Tom did not return, but he must have re-entered by the back stairway for he was abed when I retired. When I tried to explain what had happened, he again became angry, sprang from the bed and went up attic, where he remained all night, sleeping, I guess, on the old featherbed. This morning, I did not see him for he went directly to the barn.

At noontime, he was still angry at the loss of a swarm and blames me for not taking charge of Ralph's efforts. I would not be so distressed if this were the first time, but more and more he expects me to do barn work and then vehemently accuses me of incompetence when anything goes wrong. I certainly want to help him, for I know how frequently he is unwell, but I certainly cannot raise six children as they should be raised and serve as a farm hand at the same time. I also worry about his choice of associates, for I have noticed that after spending time with his war-mates, his language becomes profane and I will not have my children exposed to vulgarity.

Dear, dear sister, I should not report such things to you, but I must express my fears. I shall put this in my apron pocket and before mailing it, I will re-read it and probably destroy it. This is not the reality that an honest wife should be revealing to anybody.

I shall sign my name only after I have reconsidered. P.S. Tuesday, two days later:

Again this morning, Tom berated Ralph for losing a May swarm. I suggested that if his bees were so important to him he should stay home and take care of them. He cursed me and raised his hand as if to strike me, but again he turned and left the house. I have not set eyes on him since. I know that at heart Tom is a good man, but I am apprehensive that he neglects his children and sometimes treats his wife unfairly. I have no idea how I would clothe the children at all if it were not for the generosity of my family and the cast-offs from the neighbors and some of Tom's relatives.

I shall send Mary Emma down to Aphia's with this letter, so that Brother Jake can mail it when he goes to the Post Office tomorrow. Don't show it to anyone, but I just had to unburden myself to someone of these dreadful considerations and there is no one here I can talk to. Write me soon of your opinion.

Your devoted sister,
Elizabeth

CHAPTER 23

"It is a wonderful fact that mistakes of ignorance in the realm of motherhood may often be overcome." **Science of Feeding Babies etc.:** *H. Elizabeth Gould. Rebman Co., NY. (1916) Pg. 101.*

Three months had elapsed since Lizzie wrote to her sister about the beehive incident. There must have been a reply because correspondence between the two continued and later letters indicate that other members of the Foster family were becoming aware of Tom's harsh treatment of Lizzie and their family. However, no copy exists. Lizzie undoubtedly destroyed it.

"Are you home, Elizabeth?" Rebecca called at the back door.

"Come on in, Mother Gould," Lizzie responded from the kitchen as she recognized her mother-in-law's voice. "How do you happen to be in the neighborhood?"

"Charles said he was headin' this way, so I asked him to drop me off. He'll be back by in 'bout an hour." As she entered the kitchen, the children ran to embrace their grandmother. She picked up Franklin, the toddler, and held him in her arms. "How's Eunice?" she asked, as she was kissing each child in turn.

"Doing poorly. Mary Emma's in with her now. She's having trouble keeping her food down."

"Poor old lady. I'll go speak to her in a minute." She shook herself loose from the besieging throng and held up an envelope. "Got a letter from Levi. Thought Tom'd want to see it."

"Tom's working in the lower meadow and won't be back till dark."

"Oh, dear. I kind o' hoped he'd be here to read it to me. My eyesight ain't so good as it used to be an' there's parts of his writin' I can't make out."

"May I read it for you?"

"Tom always does, but I guess it'll be all right. I don't guess he'd mind."

Rebecca sat in the rocking chair by the window. Franklin snuggled into her lap and Louise leaned against her shoulder. Lizzie, standing nearby, began reading:

> ### Bismarck, Dakota Terr.
> ### July 30th, 1881

My Dear Mother:

We just heard out here about the President getting shot.

"My goodness," Rebecca interrupted, "That must have been at least a month ago."

"At least," Lizzie agreed. "Levi explains:"

I learned about it this morning when we drove into town for the first time in a month. It's a terrible thing. First Abe Lincoln and now Garfield. Al wants to know...

Lizzie hesitated and held the letter for Rebecca to look at.

"I think this word is 'Al'. Do you know who Al is?"

"That's Al Hinckley. He's sort o' like Levi's partner. They're homesteadin' right next to one another. Don't rightly remember where Levi met him—Boston?...or was it Leadville? Somewheres. Levi claims he's a cousin, but I don't know about that. Never heard of a cousin named Al. None of us Hinckleys ever named a boy Al that I know of. But Levi mentions him in all his letters, so I guess they make a good team."

"It's strange Tom's never mentioned any Al Hinckley to me. How long has Levi known him?"

"Oh, for ages...No good reason for Tom to mention him, be there? Ain't there more letter?"

"Certainly. Levi goes on:"

Al wants to know what Tom thinks this is going to do to Jim Blaines chances, if the President ends up passing on? A lot of folks out here think pretty highly of our secretary of state from the state of Maine. Some say he ought to be President. What does Tom think.

It's been hot out here and the wind sure blows like all get-out. Last month the wind blew so hard it blew a fellow's hat up against the side of his barn and it was up there for three days before he could get it down. Had to get a ladder to reach it and a crowbar to pry it loose.

Rebecca snickered with a high-pitched cackle.

"Tom'll get a laugh out o' that," she said. "Sure sounds just like Levi."

"It certainly does," said Lizzie, a trace of annoyance in her voice. She continued reading:

I guess you heard that Sitting Bull surrendered. Hollis (he lives a piece farther out on the prairie than us) stopped by on his way home to say they was bringing the redskins into Bismarck, so Al and me went in to see them. They was taking Sitting Bull to a place called Standing Rock, which sounds to me like a good place for him. Old Sitting Bull came riding in on an army buckboard, sitting up straight as a ramrod, with his braves all sitting around him. He is a hard looking old ticket, appeared mighty uncomfortable, especially in the outfits the army rigged them out in. Redskins out here run around without any close on, so when the army was bringing them into where civilized folks lived, they give each one of them an old uniform and made them put it on. They looked mighty strange—savages all dressed up in army uniforms. They looked even stranger when they climbed down off the buckboard. They had to back off and everyone of them had taken a knife and for convenience sake had cut the seat out of his britches.

"Why, Lizzie," Rebecca gasped. "Do you believe that?"

"He says it's true. Here's what he writes."

Thats gospel true, every word of it. I dont swear to the accuracy about the wind blowing, but the story about Sitting Bull is just the way it happened."

"I declare," said Rebecca. "What do you know about that?"

"Well," said Lizzie, "Even if it is true, I'm astonished Levi would write such a story to his mother."

"Levi probably figured Tom would be reading the letter to me and he'd get a laugh out of it. What else does he write?"

I hear the railroad is looking for masons to stone up wells along the right of way west of here where there laying track through the mountains. I figure I got things under control here, what with Al looking after things while I'm gone, so I am heading out for a few months to pick up extra money so we can buy some gear.

Dont expect to hear from me whilst I am gone because I will be out of touch, but I will write when I get a chanse.

Yr obedient son
Levi.

P.S.—enclosed find a dollar to buy raisins or something for Tom's family.

"So that's what the dollar's for," Rebecca said, taking it out of her apron pocket. "I wondered what it was for when I opened the letter. You'd be doin' a lot better, Lizzie, to spend it on shoes than on sweets. They'll be needin' shoes for school."

"No," Lizzie declared. "Their father will buy the children's shoes. When Tom goes in to town, I'll have him buy some raisins, just as Levi says. Sun-dried raisins will be nutritious for the children."

The corners of Rebecca's mouth turned down but she made no reply.

"I guess," she sighed after a brief moment, "This means Levi won't be coming home right away,"

"Not soon," Lizzie agreed and added wistfully. "How free he sounds. Just pick up and leave for the mountains to earn extra money. A man can do that sort of thing."

Eunice died in mid-October. Her coughing spells had grown increasingly severe as summer ended. There still were days when she threw off her malady and was able to greet the children by name when Lizzy sent them into her bedroom. But by late September she was too weak to recognize anyone. How her frail body withstood such wracking seizures baffled Dr. McLellan, but she continued to fight for life. He prescribed laudanum dissolved in rum. Rebecca, who volunteered no other assistance during the long siege, surprisingly procured rum. Lizzie administered the concoction day and night until the morning Mary Emma peeked into her aunt's bedroom and then ran to her mother.

"I think Aunt Eunice has stopped breathing," she sobbed.

❦   ❦   ❦

November 1, 1881

Dear Brother Caleb,

I am so grateful for your unstinted support during our recent weeks of grief. Your letters of concern have been so important to me. It has been a week since we laid Tom's half-sister Eunice to rest beside her father and mother in the village cemetery high on the hill overlooking the Androscoggin River. Thus an end was written to the suffering she has endured during her final year. She was 15 years older than Mother Gould. Until her final illness, she was a guardian angel to our children, comforting them when they scraped a knee and offering sweets to mend hurt feelings.

Tom was very fond of Eunice, who served during his childhood almost as his second mother. He has taken her death very hard. Sometimes in the struggles of day-to-day life one fails to see the compassion that lies in the hearts of others. He made all the arrangements for her funeral and burial and tenderly gave solace to the children on the death of their beloved Aunt Eunice. I was very pleased and told him so, and he promised to be a better father in the future. Even now he has several pieces of my kitchen furniture in the shed where he is repairing them whenever he gets a chance, especially my old rocking chair which was becoming unglued. Tom is an excellent carpenter, but he always depended on his brother Levi to do any cabinet work. Since Levi left for the Dakotas many of the little jobs about the house have remained untouched.

Your letters, Brother Caleb, are so ennobling and so filled with wisdom. I have finally finished "Ben Hur", which you sent early this summer. I hope you don't mind my taking so long, but I have so little time to read. I believe Tom is reading it now, although he has not said so. Since I told him it was written by General Lew Wallace, I have seen him with it on several occasions. As a consequence, I won't be able to send it on to Sister Emma until he finishes it. As you indicated in your letter, it reads almost like another Gospel, demonstrating the power of our Savior to bring peace and understanding even to the Jews who crucified Him.

Thank you so much for everything.

Your loving sister,
Elizabeth.

CHAPTER 24

✿

"So far I have treated the subject of proper feeding as if it were of most importance to women; but our boys need quite as much to be taught its precepts, if they would qualify to provide suitably for those entrusted to their care.

"A wise plan, indeed, it would be, if mothers should incorporate into their working ideal for their boys, knowledge and plans for making of them not only good sons, but good husbands.

"Some homes fail of happiness by such a sorry margin.

"Might not a similar collection of general facts for boys and girls with regard to home life help to soothe and smooth unlooked-for difficulties.

"How common now for a wife to quiet herself, and crush rebellion, by saying, 'A man simply cannot understand how a woman feels in such a matter.'

"But a man might have understood when a boy, if his mother had only believed that he could, and that he ought. It is never too late to mend, and many a man will be glad when he knows how to surround her life with a peaceful atmosphere as to prolong herdays and to bring about the best blessings to their children.

"And here we reach a very important part of our subject. As surely as boys become men, and it is not good for them to be alone, just as certainly will they make mistakes in taking proper care of their helpmeet, without instructions about, and understanding of what she needs. The best intentions will not meet the *case." **Science of Feeding Babies etc.**; H. Elizabeth Gould. Rebman Co., NY. (1916) Pg. 94.*

June 22, 1882

My Dear Sister Emma:

Although the calendar says it is only summer again, it seems as if a century has passed since summer a year ago. When I watch little Lillian struggling to walk, I am forced to realize how much has happened in the 15 months since she was born. The children, fortunately, stay healthy. After their Aunt Eunice was laid to rest, Grace and Louise began sleeping in her old chamber. Baby Franklin sleeps with his sister Mary in their grandmother's bed whenever she is not here, which these days is most of the time. Mother Gould always stays very busy. Tom, of course, has spells of discomfort, but in general the past year has been good to him. However, the farm work still has to be taken care of whenever Tom is under the weather (by myself, of course), but Ralph is getting big enough to be of help.) Indeed, Tom depends so much on Ralph I sometimes fear that the boy will be unable to complete his schooling. Also, I could not get along without Mary Emma, dear child, who is industrious both in the kitchen and in the barn.

In your latest letter you indicated that the whole Foster family has been discussing whether or not my children and I are in some danger. I can assure you that such is not the case. It is true, as you say, that I could not possibly furnish adequate food and clothing for my family without the donations of relatives and neighbors. I have remonstrated with Tom, but he, as the poet says, "not using half his store, still grumbles that he has no more." Although he insists that he is apportioning all he can afford to his family, I shall continue to plead with him for I believe he can provide better. There have been times when my words on this subject anger him, but he controls his passion through hard work. In a moment of good humor he once told me that nothing "turneth away wrath" like mowing a meadow. He never raises a hand against me and punishes the children only when they deserve it, although sometimes more severely than I warrant.

He finally repaired my rocking chair, which I believe I reported was broken, at least, in my last three letters. The rockers had become unglued so that when I rocked forward the legs lifted out of the rocker, and when I rocked back they snapped into place like a gun shot. At the time of Eunice's death Tom promised to fix several pieces of broken furniture, and although most of them still languish in the work shed, I kept after him about the rocking chair until he restored it as good as new. Not, however, without protest.

I hope you, too, have a chair as comfortable as mine. I do not know how I could get along without it. No matter how annoyed I may become with Tom's demands; no matter how exhausted I may be, either physically or spiritually, a few minutes in my rocking chair and peace descends. I am certain nothing gives a child such a feeling of security as being rocked in its mother's arms.

However, the rocking chair is my magic carpet.

Ah! What I accomplish in my imagination as I sail to and fro across my sea of dreams! I shall confess something to you and it must go no further. Recently, Brother Avery sent me a book that he had come across in his practice, entitled "The Training of Children" by Helen Hunt Jackson. He suggested that with my experience and talent I could pen an even better volume. I was very flattered, but I must admit that since he planted the seed such a project has frequented my fantasies. If only I had the opportunity to demonstrate the practicality of my theories and the time to write, I am sure that I could produce a book that would be of enormous help to young mothers everywhere. However, this will not be. I shall remain as I am, occasionally dreaming, as I rock one of my dear children to sleep, of accomplishments that are quite beyond my reach.

I am writing this letter at the kitchen table. Tom is already abed. Grace is rocking the baby in my chair. Franklin is getting a free ride on the back astraddle the two rockers and holding on for dear life. He is a real boy!

Write if you have the time. Elizabeth.

By 1882 Ralph had exhausted the resources of the one-room school at the four corners and in late August began a daily six-mile-round trek to the village school in Lisbon. It took several days for the school authorities to determine which class to put him in. For six years he had attended school, but he had learned only what his teachers knew, plus what he had learned at home from his parents and grandmother. One year his teacher had been a scholar (but also a tippler, as the town discovered) and Ralph had learned to conjugate Latin irregular verbs. The following year the school board selected a young woman from the town of Damariscotta who turned out to be incurably homesick. Ralph learned little that year except the local gossip from that seacoast village. So it went, but since each of his teachers quickly discovered the value of enforced memorizing for maintaining discipline in the multi-classed one-room school, he could recite volumes of rhymes and orations.

One night after the children were in bed, Lizzie asked:

"Tom, did Ralph tell you he's been chosen to speak a piece at his school's autumn program?"

"Ayuh."

"It sounds like quite an honor, considering he's just starting in this school."

"Ayuh."

"I'd like to get him a new jacket to wear. He really doesn't have an agreeable jacket."

"What's he need with a new jacket? Ain't the one he's got agreeable enough?"

"Oh, Tom. All he has is that old one from Caleb that I cut down for him. And that has patches on the elbows."

"What's he recitin', anyways?"

"Now, don't change the subject. I was talking about a new jacket for Ralph."

"And I was askin' what he's recitin'. What's wrong with askin' a question?"

"His recitation is the 'Landlord's Tale' from Longfellow's Tales of a Wayside Inn. He already knows every word of it. I want him to have a new jacket."

"That's the one about Paul Revere, ain't it? The one he was declaimin' to the cows this mornin' while he was milkin'"

"I believe it is." Lizzie was detecting a sound of parental pride as Tom considered Ralph's accomplishments. She continued: "And certainly he needs a new coat if he's going to stand up before our neighbors to declaim it."

"That's a good piece o' poetry. I like it. Patriotic."

It didn't work. Lizzie changed her approach to something more of a demand:

"I won't have my son appearing in front of our neighbors in that ragged old jacket."

"Stop it, Lizzie. Show some common sense."

"But what will people say?"

"They'll say, 'Tom Gould has the sense not to spend money he ain't got.'"

"You know perfectly well we can afford a new jacket for Ralph."

"Who do you think you're married to, anyways? That Rockefeller gent they was writin' about in the Journal last week? The last I heard, we ain't discovered oil on Lisbon Ridge."

"Tom Gould, I don't know what you're saving for, but it can't be more important than clothes for our children."

"Wait just a minute, now. Lizzy. You looky here. There's some things you don't understand, and money's one of 'em. You never can tell when somethin's goin' to break down on a farm and we're goin' to be needin' cash."

As if she were seeing him for the first time, Lizzy glared at Tom for a full minute, her chair rocking more and more slowly. Finally, her back stiffened. With her feet planted firmly, she brought the chair to a full stop.

"You never seem to have trouble finding money for one of your encampments," she said.

Tom seemed about to reply, but after a moment he thought better of it. In frustration he slammed his fist on the table, rose from his chair and headed for their second floor bedroom.

Lizzie rocked gently. After a few minutes she reached for a book that was lying on her sewing table nearby, but in the dim light of the lamp, she was unable to read. She wiped the moisture from her eyes, but still could not see well enough to keep her mind on the words. She got up, turned down the lamp and blew it out; then felt her way through the darkness to the back stairway.

Tom was still awake. As she climbed in beside him, he reached over and pulled her toward him.

"Gettin' and spendin' money is my affair," he said softly. "You know that, Lizzie, dear. Let's not be angry."

"And seeing that our children are properly taken care of is mine," she replied, as she pushed him away.

"Be reasonable," he beseeched, placing his hand on her breast and moving closer.

"No, Tom. You have no right."

"Husbands have a right and wives have a duty," he declared.

Helen Shaw Gould, the fifth daughter of Thomas and Elizabeth Gould, was born April 27, 1883.

BOOK THREE

"Children, if possible, should sleep in a room by themselves, and always with an open window. Oxygen, though as important as food, is often overlooked because it does not cost money." Science of Feeding Babies etc.: H. Elizabeth Gould. Rebman Co. NY. (1916) Pg. 72.

The first time Tom struck Lizzie in anger she hardly felt the blow, but for the rest of her life, whenever she recalled the incident, she put her hand to her cheek as if it still smarted. It was the unexpectedness that had staggered her. Many times she had experienced his angry outbursts, but she had attributed them (whenever it occurred to her to attempt to analyze her husband) to an affliction newspapers called "irritable heart". They said it was common among veterans of the War. She had learned to ignore Tom's flare-ups. Whenever he raised his hand as if to strike her, some inner scruple always restrained him.

Then, while she was pregnant with Helen it happened.

Before dawn Tom had harnessed Fan; then yelled from the dooryard that he was driving to Lewiston. When Lizzie asked why, he replied tersely:

"To pick up some things." Before she had time to speak again, he drove off.

She was still rankled by his surly response when later that morning she saw through the kitchen window her sister-in-law, Aphia, gingerly plodding up through the orchard. She was carrying a cane, but it was of little use in the soft earth. Lizzie was in no mood to entertain the deaf old woman, but she felt obliged to go to the back door and call to Ralph who was busy in the barnyard with the chores his father had laid out for him:

"Run down, dear, and help your aunt. She's coming up the path from her house."

Ralph stuck his dung fork in the ground and raced around the barn and down the hill. He was happy to be relieved temporarily of his responsibility. By the time the two had entered the kitchen, Aphia had revealed her errand to Ralph. His face showed that he was delighted.

"Auntie wants me to come stay with 'em," he called to his mother as they came through the doorway. "She says I can go back to school."

"We need a boy," Aphia explained to Lizzie that although Jake had rid himself of most of the farm drudgery, he still had a few chickens, a milch cow, and a small garden patch. Niah, who now lived in the village with his own family, dropped by regularly with whatever staples his parents needed and in wintertime cut firewood for their kitchen stove, but between times the old couple required young hands and a strong back. Niah's eldest, she explained, wouldn't be big enough to stay with his grandparents for at least two years. She had a bed ready for Ralph and promised to provide whatever clothes he needed.

Immediately Lizzie agreed. She decided without hesitation that her inconsiderate husband did not deserve to be consulted.

"But what'll Dad say when he gets home?" Ralph asked woefully.

"Never you mind about your father. You've got to finish your schooling. If you stay here you'll never have a chance."

"But what about my chores?"

"Now, no more 'buts'. If your father needs someone to do chores, he can hire a hand. You go get your clothes together and get down to your aunt's before your father even finds out. Let him argue with your uncle if he wants you back."

Since Ralph had little to claim as his own beside the clothes he was wearing, it took only a few minutes for him to gather his belongings.

"Aphia, you're the answer to my prayers," Lizzie shouted at her deaf sister-in-law as they waited. "I've been concerned about Ralph ever since he had to give up school. I don't know how many times I've told Tom he's giving Ralph too much to do. The boy never had time to walk all that distance into town. But Tom won't budge. He says Ralph has all the learning he needs to be a farmer. But I have other ambitions for Ralph. With Jake and you on my side, perhaps I can get Tom to listen."

Aphia nodded as if she had heard what Lizzie said.

"Well, as you say, Sister. Jake ain't good for much these days, what with his game leg and all, but I guess he and Ralph can take care of things."

By the time Tom arrived home that evening, Lizzie had rehearsed many times a speech explaining Ralph's absence. But she never had a chance to deliver it. As he drove into the yard Tom spied the dung fork sticking in the ground and quickly discerned that the manure pile he had expected to be moved was untouched.

"Where the hell is that lazy good-for-nothin'?" he shouted as he burst into the kitchen, brandishing the dung fork before him. The children, eating supper, looked up from the table apprehensively. Louise, who sat near the door, flinched as her father strode by.

"Don't bring that dirty thing into my kitchen," Lizzie ordered.

Tom scrutinized the object in his hand as if he'd forgotten why he was carrying it and, then, in a rage slammed it to the floor.

"Damn your kitchen," he shouted. "Where's Ralph?" Hunks of moist cow manure broke from the vibrating tines and scattered across the floor and against the wall.

"Tom Gould, don't you talk to me that way." Lizzie stepped forward, her eyes blazing, and placed herself directly in his path.

He struck her, but, even as he swung, his fist opened so that instead of punching, as seemed his intention, he merely slapped her face. And the compunction that had restrained his anger in the past, now slowed his arm. The blow scarcely reddened her cheek.

They stood glaring at each other.

"Ralph has gone," she said at last.

"Wha'd'ya mean? Gone?"

"I cannot discuss it now," she sobbed and burst into tears. She fled across the kitchen to the bedchamber where her mother-in-law slept whenever she was at the farm. Lizzie remembered that the old lady had insisted on having a lock put on her door. She slammed the door and turned the key.

"Where's he gone? What've you done with him?" Tom yelled, as he grabbed the latch and pushed his shoulder against the door. The children watched in silent amazement. Tom stood frustrated, too angry to turn away, yet too frugal to break down the door, until finally Grace disclosed primly:

"Ralph's gone down to live with Aunt Aphia and Uncle Jake. He took his clothes and everything. He's goin' back to school."

In the end Lizzie won this argument. She had anticipated that Tom would not want to buck his older brother. For several nights she slept in Rebecca's room but during the day went about her housework as if nothing had happened. Tom came into the house only for meals and sleeping. He spoke very little, addressing his wife through the children.

"Mary Emma," he would say, "Ask your mother what time supper'll be ready."

But in a few days, Ralph stopped by on his return from school. He talked to his mother for a while and then, at her suggestion, went to the barn to see his father.

"How're you an' your uncle gittin' along?" Tom asked.

"Just fine," said Ralph.

"Back in school?"

"Ayuh."

"That's good," said his father.

When Tom came into the house at suppertime, he asked Lizzie if Ralph had been by to visit and she said yes. When Tom went to bed that evening he found Lizzie there ahead of him.

But in another sense, Lizzie lost, for Ralph lasted only a couple of months at Jake's. He relished being out from under his father's control. When he heard that a farmer living a few miles down the river in Pejepscot was looking for a boy to help with his livestock, he decided that he had learned enough to last him a lifetime and applied for the job. His schooling came to an end.

One day about a month after the birth of Helen, Tom called from the doorway of the barn.

"Lizzie, come out here! I need you!"

She was busy in the kitchen. The baby had been fed and was asleep in the crib in the corner. Lillian was napping on the couch under the enclosed stairway to the second floor. All the older children were at school. *(See note at end of chapter)*

When Lizzie failed to answer, Tom called again, louder and with his hands cupping his mouth. Still he got no reply. He moved out into the dooryard and yelled a third time. At length, he climbed the back steps and pounded on the door.

"What the devil are you doin'? Can't you hear me?"

She came to the door.

"Yes, I hear you. What do you want?"

"If you heared me, whyn't you come?"

"I said I hear you. I didn't say I heard you."

Tom's anger was rising and Lizzie's reply did nothing to mollify him.

"Come on. I need you in the barn," he shouted vehemently, backing down the steps.

"You don't have to raise your voice." She stood with her hand on the door latch as if she planned to close it again. "You'll just have to wait. I can't leave the babies alone."

"Woman," he cried, "You're opposin' me."

"That I am," she said as calmly as she could and she stepped back into the kitchen.

He bounded up the steps, placed his foot against the door to keep it from closing, and grabbed Lizzie by the wrist. With a jerk she pulled herself loose and stumbled against the kitchen table, toppling it over, dishes and all. Lillian, wakened by the crash, started to cry.

"Damn you," he snapped. "When I say I need you, I need you." He grabbed her wrist again and pulled her toward him, circling her neck with his right arm. He began dragging her through the doorway. She clutched at the jamb.

"You're choking…me," she gasped. "Let me…go."

Helen woke and added her wails to her sister's screams. Lizzie suddenly let go of the door casing and stopped resisting. Tom found himself standing on the top step with his wife behind him, her head locked under his arm, and the two children shrieking in the background. Looking toward the road, he saw a horse and buggy coming up the hill with a man and woman in it. He didn'twait to learn whether they would turn into his yard.

He released Lizzie. She straightened; her face was flushed and she was out of breath, but she had suffered no injury.

"You may go back to the barn now," she said meekly and stepped back into the kitchen.

He watched the couple, who he now realized were strangers, as they continued up the hill.

"Damn her," he said aloud. "I'll just take care of things myself."

He headed toward the barn.

Note: Franklin had already started school at three and a half. When Louise became old enough to enter the first grade, he found himself alone at home. Lillian was too tiny to be much of a playmate. The second day of classes he followed his older sisters up the hill to the school house. His mother, glancing out her kitchen window, was just in time to see him disappearing into the schoolyard. She waited for one of the older girls to bring him home, but none did. She called to Tom but he was out of hearing. Finally, with Helen on her shoulder and Lillian by the hand, she went to fetch her wandering boy.

He was sitting in the front row. The girls had begged the teacher to let him stay, but she had insisted that no child could come to school unless he knew his alphabet. Grace set her jaw with determination.

"He knows his ABC's!" she declared. She dragged Franklin to the front of the room and ordered him to recite his letters. With great assurance he eyed the roomful of students and began:

> *"Great A, little A, bouncing B,*
> *the cat's in the cupboard*
> *and can't C me."*

The teacher decided that this was even better than knowing the alphabet and had assigned Franklin a seat.

CHAPTER 26

"Is your child inclined to constipation? Give natural acids, such as orange juice and raw apples. For a young child apples should be scraped but they are always gratefully received by a child in normal condition of six months old. A child's food before one year old should be mostly milk, supplemented with entire wheat bread, fruit juices, potato and egg. After that meat broths and gravy are valuable additions, gradually taking in a little meat, but sparingly, for your child can thrive and grow if it has no meat." **Science of Feeding Babies etc.: H. Elizabeth Gould.** *Rebman Co., NY. (1916) Pg. 73.*

July 8, 1883

My Dear Sister Lizzie:

I don't know what to say. When I got your letter yesterday I just wept. What is a mother to do when the father of her children so misuses her? And even in front of the children themselves. I have always believed that Tom is unreasonable, yes, even cruel, when he makes you do the heavy work in the barn, especially those times when you have been in a family way. And in spite of your protestations, I have felt all along that Tom has not provided for his family as well as he could and should. He is a hard, miserly man. But you must be strong, sweet Lizzie. The children need your strength. You have all my sympathy and love, but I cannot advise you otherwise. Although I sometimes find my own life difficult, I have always at my side someone with whom I can share my burden.

Have you written to Brother Caleb? You should, but when you do, ask only his counsel. Do not mention that you have considered leaving Tom for that would distress him. He is wise and so familiar with the teachings of our Savior. If he can do no more, he will provide you with the solace of the Scriptures. If you have not already written to him, I hope you will do so at once. Meanwhile, rest assured that the tribulations you have divulged to me shall travel no farther than my eyes. I will not add to your distress. Know my prayers are with you always.

But do, I beseech you, write to Caleb.

Your loving sister.
Emma.

❦   ❦   ❦

**Methodist Parsonage
Northwood, N. Hamp.
July 18, 1883**

My Dear Lizzie:

I received your letter only this afternoon and I shall not wait to reply. Previously, members of our family have described the hardships that the Almighty has allotted to you, but I had no notion that you might be facing physical danger. The Lord is requiring you to carry a heavy burden, dear Sister. Life is seldom easy for any of His flock, but in His wisdom He sometimes selects one individual, as He did with Job, and tries the very substance of a soul. Your letter leaves me heartsick that I do not live close enough to visit and pray with you, as I have so many times with those in my parish who face like challenges to their faith. Indeed, if it may be of any solace, know that you are not alone. Many times am I called upon to strengthen the faith of wives (and husbands) who face far greater trials than you can imagine.

Lizzie, dear, you must accept that the Lord has called you to be a mother. You have seven fine and healthy children. There is no greater summons for a woman than to minister to her family. Sometimes in your letters I fear I have discerned that you desire the independence to pursue a more stimulating vocation. You must forgo such thoughts. I would not suggest that any wayward thought on your part excuses Tom's recent actions, but when the wife is creating a warm and loving home, the husband can respond only with appreciation. Give up any dream that might cause Tom to doubt your dedication to your family.

Searching my Bible for a message of import for you, I was led as if by God's bidding to the "Epistle to the Romans", where Paul writes: "The woman who hath a husband is bound by the law to her husband as long as he liveth." Read Chapter 7. You will find much to ponder. Or turn to Matthew, Chap. 19, where Jesus replies to the Pharisees who have questioned Him about the duties of husband and wife. They are "no more twain, but one flesh," He declares. One finds abundant wisdom in Scripture.

Have you spoken with your own pastor? Although I have conversed briefly with him, I do not know the Rev. Mr. Plummer very well, but he has certainly served his parish long and diligently. I believe, if I remember correctly, it was he who performed your wedding ceremony. The Gould family has long attended his church. I am sure that he can provide comfort and, perhaps, open unto you more wisdom and inspiration than I have been able to tender in this brief letter.

Humble in the service of our Savior
Your loving brother Caleb.

Lizzie was uncertain that a conversation with the elderly preacher of her church would produce any benefit. His sermons had become perfunctory. Frequently, when his mind wandered as he looked up from his notes, he had difficulty finding his place. But she knew he was a good man. And she respected the opinion of her older brother, even though the content of his latest letter hardly offered acceptable solutions to any of her problems.

Weekly she planned that after church services she would ask the Reverend to call on her, but, instead, over and again she would only smile at him as she left the sanctuary, shake his hand and, perhaps, say she had been moved by his sermon. Sundays when Tom was standing nearby, she was afraid that making the request would arouse his anger. When they had brought Tom's mother to church with them, Lizzie was reluctant to speak to the preacher for fear her mother-in-law would ask questions she didn't want to answer. But most often, she refrained from speaking because at the last moment she decided that sooner or later Tom's hostility would disappear if she ignored it long enough. She had read that "irritable heart" and other afflictions common to veterans become less pronounced as memories of the war fade.

Months went by. Much of the time life with Tom was bearable. After a day in the field, he would return to the house tired and hungry. Silently he would eat his supper and soon retire for the night. Lizzie longed for stimulating conversation, but tried to be satisfied that what words were exchanged were uncritical. He frequently did show affection for the children, even though he balked at spending money on their clothes.

He enjoyed taking them to G.A.R. field days and parades and proudly took credit when they excelled at games or contests. At other times, however, he barked angrily at them for being noisy when he was "trying to rest" or for making "careless mistakes", such as pulling up a seedling instead of a weed. She intervened when she felt he was punishing a child too severely, even at the risk that he might turn on her again, as frequently he threatened to do.

Emergencies were the times she dreaded. No matter how tired or ill she might be, how busy with her household duties, or how involved with one of the children, when Tom declared an "emergency", as he did all too regularly, she was expected to drop everything and rush to assist. When a hog broke loose from the sty, or a cow had difficulty calving, or a sudden shower threatened to drench a load of hay—these and many other happenings would evoke a bellow from Tom:

"Lizzie, come here." In the heat of August or when the icy blasts of January crackled the rafters of the old house, he required a quick and unhesitating response.

Another summer came. One morning in late June while Lizzie was feeling particularly miserable because she feared she was pregnant for the eighth time, she saw through the kitchen window the Rev. Mr. Plummer turn his little horse into her dooryard. He was making his annual parish call.

Earlier Tom had harnessed Fan to the wagon and left for the day without telling her where he was going.

Several times that morning she had told Grace to stop nagging Louise, until, exasperated, she had sent them both outside. She could hear them still bickering. Mary Emma was trying to attend to Franklin and Lillian who both had runny noses and were whining for their mother and, despite their older sister's efforts, tugging at their mother's skirt. Baby Helen was crying to be changed. It had been several weeks since she had seen or even heard from Ralph. If ever a woman needed solace this was the day.

"Mary Emma," she commanded, "Make some tea. You've got to take charge for a while. Keep the children quiet. I'm talking with the Reverend Plummer in the other room and I don't want to be disturbed. I'll tell you when to bring in the tea."

She removed her apron, ran her hand over her forehead to smooth back her hair, and, closing the kitchen door behind her, rushed to the front door before The Reverend had a chance to knock. She ushered him into the parlor.

"I am so very glad to see you, my dear Mr. Plummer," she exclaimed. "So very glad! I have many things to discuss with you."

She grasped his hand and motioned him toward the sofa Rebecca had purchased when she married Tom's father, the only cushioned chair in the room. The preacher, somewhat startled by the effusive warmth of her reception, sat stiffly.

"Many things?" he repeated.

"Yes, yes. Many things."

Before she could go on, tears welled into her eyes and she began to sob. He took her hand as she sat beside him.

"Now, now," he said.

Several times she tried to speak, but her sobs prevented her saying anything coherent. Finally, she blurted out that she had no other choice than to leave her husband. The clergyman, staggered by such an announcement, released her hand as though it were contaminating and stood up. He stroked his snowy beard, lowered the pitch of his voice to a funereal level, and boomed:

"Mrs. Gould, do you realize what you are saying? Think of your children."

"Yes," she said but she could say no more. She could think only of the probability that in nine months she would have another. She rose and crossed to the window. As soon as she was able to control her voice she would tell him the whole story of the nightmare she was living.

"I left my Bible in the carriage," he said. "I'll fetch it and we'll read together."

Lizzie closed her eyes to shut out the sight of the broad landscape she had once thought so beautiful.

"Eunice's Bible is on the stand," she suggested without turning. "Will that do?"

"Aye, yes."

He picked up the Book and turned quickly to a passage that, it can be assumed, he had referred to many times before.

"Sit down, my child." His voice was again ministerial. "Let us consider together this message from Paul's Epistle to the Ephesians."

"Yes," she sighed as she slipped meekly into a straight-backed chair nearby.

"Chapter Five, verse twenty-two," he announced and began to intone. "'Wives submit yourselves unto your own husbands as unto the Lord.'"

"'Submit', does it say?" she interrupted. "Why should wives submit?"

"Let us not discuss this until I have finished the reading," he directed. "The scripture continues, verse twenty-three: 'For the husband is the head of the wife, even as Christ is the head of the church; and he is the savior of the body. Therefore as the church is subject unto Christ, so let the wives be to their own husbands in every thing.'" He paused, more to allow her to consider the wisdom of the injunction than to offer her an opportunity to reply. But she had heard enough. She strode to the front door and threw it open.

"Mr. Plummer," she said. "You need read no more. I have listened to all I wish to hear. Good day."

"But, my child," he protested.

"I must see to my children," she said. She crossed to the kitchen and closed the door behind her. He started to follow but after a couple of steps thought better of it. In a moment she heard the squeak of the wheels as the preacher's carriage pulled out of the dooryard.

CHAPTER 27

Gentleness is a far more effectual teacher than harshness, if we could only remember it, but a child learns very quickly whether your voice indicates gentle firmness or easy slackness. A baby easily becomes a tyrant, but it is never the baby's fault. A well-fed baby is naturally a delight in a household, not excepting the nights." **Science of Feeding Babies etc.:** *H. Elizabeth Gould. Rebman Co. NY. (1916) Pg. 45*

Standing by the side window of the kitchen with baby Helen asleep on her shoulder, Lizzie bleakly watched her older daughters digging potatoes in the garden beyond the barn. That morning their father had come upon the three girls showing the smaller children how to make a cat's cradle with yarn and he loudly proclaimed that he would not abide idle hands. That he had found such difficult work for them as punishment was not distressing Lizzie so much as the disagreeable tone with which he had ordered them to stop wasting time. The suspicion that he had used "sloth" as an excuse to get his daughters to do work he was unwilling to do himself re-echoed in her mind. Now, even four-year-old Franklin was following his sisters with a shortsack picking up the potatoes they uncovered.

Because of her preoccupation with her children, she had not seen her frail sister-in-law approaching at a snail's pace through the orchard. Abruptly, Aphia pushed open the kitchen door and entered.

"Lizzie, what's all this palaverin' I been hearin' 'bout you leavin' Tom?" she demanded.

Lizzie was startled—as much by the unexpected visit as by the brusque question. It had been weeks since Aphia had dropped in on her.

"Whatever do you mean?" she asked in a loud whisper. She put her finger to her lips as she spoke and nodded toward Lillian who was napping on the couch nearby. But Aphia, growing deafer with each passing year, did not hear the question. Ignoring even the gesture for quiet, she went on in her shrill voice:

"You heard about Bess Rounds passin' along, didn't you?"

Lizzie nodded. She glanced at Lillian and saw that her eyes were now open.

"I couldn't get to the funeral," she shouted in Aphia's ear. "Tom was…"

"That's what I suspected," Aphia interrupted. "Well, Jake drove me inta the services. We could of took you if I'd a knowed you didn't have some way o' gittin' there…But then, that's a whole 'nother story. I was surprised your sister Emma wan't there, but I guess she's gotten her own family to worry about these days. She sent over a nice wreath, I must say. It was put right next to the casket."

"I wondered whether Emma might come over," Lizzie said.

"What'd you say?"

"I thought Emma might be there," she shouted.

"Oh…Well, I'd no sooner gotten there than Delia Bailey sashayed up to me and asked me right out of the clear blue why you was leavin' Tom."

Lizzie shuddered. If Delia Bailey had spoken loud enough for Aphia to hear, nobody in the gathering could have missed her question.

"So I tell her I don't know anything about that," Aphia continued. "When I said that, she come back with: that was what Irma Plummer said you told her husband."

Lizzie gasped and shook her head angrily.

"I don't believe I said any such thing, Sister Aphia," she snapped. "And if I did, the Reverend Plummer has no business repeating it…to his wife or anybody else. Whatever I said to him was in confidence."

"Well, you ain't really thinkin' o' walkin' out on Tom, be ye? Not that I'd blame y' if y' did."

"I don't wish to discuss it," Lizzie retorted loud enough for Aphia to hear and turned her back on her sister-in-law.

"I didn't know things had come to such a fix, Lizzie," Aphia said gently, then added: "Well, I just figured I better tell you what folks was sayin'. From what I heared, it's all over town."

"I suppose it is," Lizzie agreed, taking a handkerchief from her apron pocket and wiping her eyes. She turned back slowly. "Of course, Aphia, I'm not leaving Tom," she declared. "We're expecting another baby in early March. You can tell that to anyone who's spreading stories about me."

"In March, eh? I figured as much, when I seen ye standin' there by the winder."

❦   ❦   ❦

Finally Aphia left. When later Mary Emma came in with Franklin and reported tartly that all the potatoes her father had left in the ground had been dug, Lizzie was still furious—not at Aphia but at the preacher and his gossiping wife.

Mary Emma immediately sensed indignation in her mother's face and manner. She fell silent and clapped her hand over Franklin's mouth. Since she had learned that her mother was again pregnant and suffering much discomfort, she was particularly heedful of her mood changes. Several mornings lately, Lizzie had had to remain in bed because of dizziness and, as she said, "squeamish stomach".

"Go wash your hands, both of you," Lizzie ordered. Mary Emma pumped water for Franklin, and they dried their hands on the roller towel back of the pantry door.

Lizzie brusquely handed the baby to Mary. Striding to the stove, she snatched up the boiling kettle and carried it to the sink. She poured hot water into a basin. She pumped enough cold to cool it, grabbed a bar of homemade soap and began to scrub the pots standing on the drain board. Mary Emma watched in dismay, then took Franklin by the hand and led him to the couch where Lillian was now fully awake.

"Shhh, all of you," she whispered.

Soon Helen began showing signs of hunger. Mary Emma recognized it was hardly the moment to call her mother's attention to this need. She carried the baby to the rocking chair. Cooing softly, she began to rock and Helen hushed. Lillian climbed on Mary's knee and snuggled against her unoccupied shoulder. Franklin approached and gazed at his baby sister, sleeping peacefully and now sucking her thumb. Mary Emma reached toward him with her free hand and swiped at his dripping nose with a cloth she had taken from her pocket. She slowed her rocking so that he could climb aboard the rockers and get the free ride he enjoyed so much.

Grace and Louise peeked in from outside. When they saw their mother was busy at the sink, they ventured to enter. When there was no sign of either greeting or disapproval, they boldly advanced. Louise climbed into a chair by the table. Grace crossed to Mary Emma.

"Let me rock Helen…please," she begged her sister.

"Not now."

She watched for a spell. Then, in a quite different tone she spoke to Franklin.

"Let me ride," she ordered. "It's my turn."

"No, it's not," he replied, taking a tighter grip on the back of the chair.

Grace stepped on the right rocker and tried to pry Franklin's fingers free. Her additional weight tilted the chair and Mary Emma leaned in the opposite direction to steady it.

"Stop it, Grace," Mary cried. "Mother, make Grace stop,"

Suddenly there was a loud snap and the rocker under Grace's foot broke at the mortise where the rear leg was connected. Grace landed in a heap on the floor. Franklin, hanging on for dear life, pulled the chair over in the opposite direction, dumping Mary Emma, Lillian and the baby. Lizzie rushed from the sink and grabbed Helen from Mary Emma's arms. The baby was unhurt, but Lillian had started to cry.

For a moment, Lizzie had something on her mind other than her reputation in town.

＊   ＊   ＊

Lizzie had been correct about the whole town now knowing of her conversation with the Reverend. When her ten-year-old daughter Grace came home the next day from playing with her friend Alice Porter, she announced that she was going to live with the Porters after her mother and father separated. Mrs. Porter had said she could. Lizzie immediately set her daughter straight.

"I have no plans for leaving your father and you may tell Mrs. Porter so."

Actually, Mrs. Porter had made no such offer. She had queried Grace to find out all she could about the quarreling Goulds. When she found Grace knew very little she dropped the subject. But Grace had thus learned of her mother's distress with her married life. She and Alice were fascinated with the prospect of Grace being abandoned and concocted the invitation. Grace, who longed to put an end to the present arrangement that she regarded as responsible for her working when she would rather be playing, felt the invitation had more authority coming from the mother.

"Tom, you promised to mend my chair," Lizzie said one evening a few days later as Tom was heading up to bed. She was making her statement sound as casual as she was able.

"Ain't had time yet. Wha'd you expect? You know I been up to my ears fittin' up firewood for winter."

Lizzie thought it best to ignore his response.

"I'm afraid my chair's going to have to have a new rocker."

"Hain't got the tools to make a new rocker. I'll have to fix the busted one. It'd take a real furniture maker and his fancy lathes to turn out a rocker anything like the whole one on the other side."

"I don't believe the old rocker can be repaired. It was broken into two pieces. You'll have to get me a new chair."

"You got that kind o' money. I hain't. I'll put a brace on it just as soon as I git a chance. You'll have to make it do."

"Tom, I need that chair to rock the baby."

"Just as soon as I git a chance." He slammed the door behind him as he started up the stairs to bed.

She rushed across the kitchen, swung open the door and yelled:

"Tom, I mean it. If you don't mend my chair tomorrow, I'll take the children and go home to Gray."

"When I git a chance," he called back.

Sometime during the night Tom decided it was wise not to test his wife's threat. In the morning as soon as his barn chores were finished, he scoured the shed for a suitable piece of lumber, finally turning up an ash strip about a foot long. Although it was wider than the rocker, it could be fitted across the break in such a way as not to interfere with rocking. Lest driving a nail might split either the rocker or the brace, he lined up the pieces and bored holes through them in several places. He found a single bolt and nut to hold one end, which he secured with leather washers. When he could locate no other bolts that fit, he fastened the rest of the holes with short lengths of fence wire, pulled tight with his pliers and twisted together on top of the rocker. He brought the chair into the kitchen.

"If you ain't too blame persnickety, here's your chair, good as new," he announced, dropping it on the floor and rocking it back and forth.

Lizzie was hardly elated but she realized this outcome was probably the best she could expect.

"Why, thank you, Tom," she said, placing her hand on the back of the chair.

"S'what you wanted, ain't it?"

She sat down. It rocked, but with a clack and a squeal as the joints rubbed together. The broken rocker tipped further than its mate, not only tilting the chair to the right as it rocked but carrying it on a circular path across the floorboards. She looked down at the repair job and wondered how many times the children would scratch themselves on the exposed wire ends.

"Do you think it will hold together all right?" she asked hesitantly. She didn't want to seem ungrateful.

"'Sup to you. If you let the young uns clamber all over it the way you been doin', it ain't goin' to last long. Take care of it and it's good as it ever was."

By the time Edgar Winfield Gould, their eighth child, had arrived a few days earlier than anticipated on the 28th of February, 1885 (little Lillian's fourth birthday), the chair was barely usable. The break had splintered so that the two pieces no longer fit together. The wires had loosened and the rear segment of the rocker flopped against the floor. The chair tilted so far to the right that for several days before it finally collapsed Lizzie could use it only if she planted her foot firmly on the floor to prevent its toppling over.

CHAPTER 28

"In almost every household babies are held more than is necessary, yet they enjoy it, and where there are enough to do it, the same enjoyment may be mutual.

"This is a good rule. If the baby is comforted and made good by being held, very well; but let no one weary herself trying to please a fretful baby. Very likely it needs a good cry, and if it persists in fretting, lay it down and let it cry. This may be hard to bear. In that case leave it alone for ten minutes, and you will find the baby feels improved for several hours by the exercise. Be sure to leave the room while you can still smile at the baby." **Science of Feeding Babies etc.: H. Elizabeth Gould. Rebman Co. NY.** *(1916) Pg. 44.*

When Lizzie insisted early in her pregnancy that her misery was more than the usual morning queasiness, Tom sent their daughters Grace and Louise up the hill to the Baker place to ask his mother to come home and take care of their mother. Rebecca sent back word that she was too old and not well. She recommended Tom call the doctor.

"In a couple of days, Lizzie, you'll probably feel better," was Tom's answer.

A week or so later when Charlie Baker was driving into town, he brought Rebecca by the farm to see her grandchildren. She had grown so frail he had to help her into the house. When she saw how pale Lizzie was and unsteady on her feet, she immediately directed Charlie to hurry to the village and send Dr.

McLellan out to the farm. The doctor put Lizzie to bed, and told Tom that she should have complete rest or she might lose the child.

Thirteen year old Mary Emma came into her mother's bedroom.

"Don't worry about the family, Mother," she said. "They'll be all right. Helen and Lillie are asleep. If they wake up I can hear them. Grace is over to the Porters and the other two are out in the back meadow building a snow house. Now, I tell you this because I want you to know that I take being a substitute mother serious. I may not be very old but I want you to be able to leave the children with me and not worry about them. I want you to get better and you may have to go live with Aunt Sarah or Aunt Emma for a while where you can rest. I don't want you worrying about the family."

"Why Mary Emma. Those are nicest words you could say to me, but I must tell you that I'm going to be all right. I feel better every day and there's nobody I would rather leave my children with than you."

When Lizzie wrote to her older sister that her condition obliged her to take to her bed and leave Mary Emma in charge of the household, Emma passed the information on to their father. Moses, now 73 and in ill-health, secured enough money from his other children to send train fare to his youngest daughter Eliza in northern Maine, who had trained as a nurse at the Massachusetts General Hospital in Boston. He instructed her to "go up" to Lisbon and stay with her sister until after the baby was born.

Eliza Foster Clark (26), married and with a family of her own, was now living in Bradford, Maine, a small town several miles north of Bangor. She asked her mother-in-law to take care of her children and on the Monday morning after Christmas left for Lisbon Ridge.

The circumstances in which she found her sister's family appalled her. She made a list of the things she wanted corrected but first told Tom that he was not leaving enough wood in the woodbox to keep fires in both the kitchen and Lizzie's bedroom.

"Whose fault is that?" he demanded.

"I believe it's the husband's duty to provide."

"A man's only gut two hands. There just weren't time enough fer me to fit up the wood to keep both fires goin' all winter. If a man's wife keeps thinkin' up damfool things for him to do when he's gittin' out the winter's firewood, whose fault is it? Besides, didn't she send her boy off someplace to split up firewood for strangers? If you want the wood to last you'll have to stint in Lizzie's bedroom. Her damned fireplace eats up too much wood anyhow."

"Well, I never," Eliza exclaimed. "Listen to that windhowling. Before morning the temperature's going to drop below zero. Tom Gould, as long as I'm here, I plan to keep Lizzie's bedroom warm."

"The house is full o' blankets. Eunice spent most of her old age weavin'. Tell Lizzie to pull up a blanket."

"Tom, she's not well."

"Let her come out here an' set by the kitchen stove. Wrap her up in a blanket. That'll warm her up."

"If you don't bring in more wood, I'll just take Lizzie some place where she can be warm."

"What's the matter with her, anyways? She never made trouble like this with the other babies. Look at this room! It never looked like this when my mother was keepin' house. Eunice never let it git this way." He swept his hand across the mantel behind the stove and held it out for Eliza to see the soot and dust on his fingers. "This place is a god-damned dirty hole."

"Don't you swear at me, Tom Gould," Eliza commanded angrily. "Tell me where the wood's kept and I'll go get it myself."

"I'll git ye some. To keep peace."

After that, Eliza avoided conversation with Tom. When the woodbox emptied, she sent one of the girls to replenish the supply. She kept the fire burning in Lizzie's fireplace as well as in the kitchen stove and prayed that the weather would moderate and the rest of the winter would be mild. To her surprise Tom put up no argument, even as the pile in the woodshed dwindled.

Luckily, Eliza's prayers were effective. Spring came early that year.

As soon as possible after Edgar was born, Eliza went home to Bradford and her own family. Not, however, until after she had written to her father:

"…Now, the time has come when I must return to my own children, but before I can leave I must beseech you, dear Father, to watch over our beloved Hannah Elizabeth. If you cannot go to her yourself, send someone you trust, preferably some member of our family, to make sure that she is all right. At least once a week.

"If it were only practical for her to go home to Gray till she has fully regained her strength! However, I know that is impossible. Lizzie and I have discussed it, but she is a devoted mother who would never leave her family—'There is no underground railway out of my slavery,' she said even when I suggested she could trust the children for a brief time to the care of Mary Emma, who is such an exceptional child (young lady).

"Tell Mother that Lizzie is doing well, recovering from a very difficult term much more rapidly than I had ever expected. Little Edgar Winfield is such a happy baby and gaining every day. The older children are also doing fine, healthy as trout, due, no doubt, to their mother's care. I declare my instructors at nursing school were no more knowledgeable on child rearing and nutrition than Lizzie.

"I have to report that Tom Gould is delighted with his new son. When I first arrived here, I found Tom's behavior to be abominable, but since the baby came I must say that he has acted much more as a husband and father should act. Nevertheless, that fact adds only to my concern. Although Dr. McLellan has told Tom that it is unsafe for Lizzie to bear another child, and I wholeheartedly agree with him, everything Tom says or does indicates that he is more interested in serving his own needs than in protecting the health of his wife. On this point, Lizzie also is apprehensive.

"I will not feel content until I know that someone is keeping an eye on my sister's well-being…"

Moses immediately sent back word to Eliza that he would be diligent in carrying out her wishes.

Fortunately, when the rocking chair finally toppled over, Lizzie was not in it. Edgar had finished nursing and had gone to sleep and she had risen gingerly from the rickety seat to deposit him in his crib. She was halfway across the kitchen when Louise and Franklin both attempted to climb into the chair. Each was clambering aboard and loudly ordering the other to desist when Grace chose to intervene. "Stop it," she ordered as she vigorously pulled the chair away from them. Sidewise motion was more than it could tolerate. The ash splint, that Tom had fashioned, fractured; the broken rocker again fell to pieces; rungs between the legs dropped out; and the seat, which had been functioning under great lopsided tension, split down the middle.

Tom picked this moment to come into the house. Lizzie with the sleeping Edgar in her arms stood surveying the wreckage in dismay. Mary Emma held out her hands to the younger children as if to gather them together before a tornado struck, but they were ignoring her invitation. With open mouths they stared at the wreckage, then from one parent to the other. Tom was the first to speak.

"Can't you take care of anything?" he roared in disgust. "When I fixed it, I figgered you couldn't take care of it. Now you'll just have to git along without your damned chair. Where do you think I'm goin' to gaffle onto the money to pay for a new one?"

Lizzie said nothing. At that instant she resolved that, come what may, she was leaving Tom—forever. How she would do it, she had no plan. When? Perhaps not today but she was going to find an escape. With a sudden confidence that things were going to be better, she placed Edgar in his crib and tucked the blankets around him. She picked up the pieces of the broken rocker and the loose rungs and put them in the wood box.

"Tom," she said calmly. "When you break up the rest of the chair I'll burn it in the stove."

The next morning Tom left early. When she had arisen Lizzie noticed the lantern burning in the stable and a few minutes later she heard the clomp of Fan's hooves as the wagon left the dooryard. She had no idea where he was going. Since it was Sunday, no one in the community was doing business. It was too early for church, even in the unlikely event that that was his plan. She shrugged with indifference. About ten o'clock she heard a wagon. She didn't bother to look out for she assumed it would be Tom returning. There was a knock at the front door.

"Mary Emma, you see who it is," she said. "Tell them your father isn't home. I don't want to see anyone." She stepped into the pantry.

"Uncle Howard, what are you doing here?" she heard Mary Emma squeal. It was Lizzie's brother, there to keep his father's promise to Eliza. Tears and sobs overwhelmed Lizzie at the realization that here was her escape route—the "underground railway out of her slavery." As Howard came through the door she dashed across the kitchen and clasped him in her arms.

"Hallelujah," she cried, "You've come to take me home."

❦   ❦   ❦

Within a half hour she had stuffed her clothing and garments for the two babies into a carpet bag, given instructions to the other children to obey Mary Emma, kissed and hugged each of them as she promised to be back as soon as possible to take them to live with her in a better home forever. She cradled Edgar on her left arm, and gave her right hand to toddling Helen.

"I'm ready," she said to her brother, her head high and her jaw resolute. Howard was not sure what to make of his sister's decision, so he chose to remain quiet.

The children watched from the dooryard as their Uncle Howard drove off with their mother and the two babies—none of them, not even frightened Mary Emma, comprehending the full import of the moment. Grace was sniv eling because she couldn't go too. Lillian was crying for her mother to stay. Louise led Franklin over to Aunt Eunice's flower bed and showed him the crocuses she had seen poking through. When he picked one she scolded him. Mary Emma could not imagine what she would tell her father when he came home.

It was April 26th, 1885, and Edgar Winfield Gould was not yet two months old.

❦   ❦   ❦

Early that afternoon, Tom returned. Mary Emma, struggling to keep back her tears, went to the stable, where he was unharnessing Fan, to give him the dreadful news. Before she could speak, he said:

"Tell your mother I got her a new chair. It don't look like much, but I guess it's sturdy enough." He pointed to a platform rocker in the back of the wagon.

CHAPTER 29

"Fear seems to underlie nearly all the troubles with which a baby has to contend. First it is feared that it may have a weak stomach, and it is tested with very weak food (the sure way to make a strong stomach weak), with the fallacious reasoning, 'if it takes care of this, all right; we can strengthen it later.' When the baby begins to fail, the same kind of reasoning says, 'Why, it cannot even digest food as strong as this; we must add more limewater'.

"It is 'feared' that a child will distend its stomach unnaturally if allowed to eat all it wants. A child that is fed regularly upon suitable food will never be hungry enough to eat to excess." **Science of Feeding Babies etc.:** *H. Elizabeth Gould. Rebman Co. NY. (1916) Pg. 27.*

May 8, 1885

Dear Rachel,

Remember me? Ruth Holmes (I married Johnny Adams} How are you these days?

You got to answer this letter rite away & tell me all you hear about Lizzie Foster—she used to be a Foster—now her name is Gould. I ran into her this morning with a couple of babies rite here in Gray, parading along the street as big as old Cuffy—naturally, I guessed something must of happened to her father, since he aint been so good lately—but she said no he was better—then I asked her about the rest of her fambly & she begun to cry & first she says she dont know & then she dont want to talk about it & finally she tells me she left them in Lisbon—then she picks up her little girl & with a baby on each shoulder she hightails it for her fathers place. Well—I asked all over town if anybody knows whats going on, but nobody seems to know. Then Thelma Bensen says why dont you write a letter to Rachel Thurlow, she would know. Wye—she said—she lives rite there in Lisbon Fls rite next door to Lizzie & they used to go to school together here in Gray when they was girls—so I said thats what Im going to do. you used to be real chummy with Lizzie. I dont have nothing against Lizzie, but she used to be so high & mighty its hard to believe she would run off & leave her fambly—one time when we was little we had some sort a fracas & Lizzie told me that her mother was a Humphrey—just like that settled the matter. i should like to know who she thinks the Humphreys are anyway.

In haste
Ruth Adams

❀   ❀   ❀

Lisbon Falls, Maine
May 1885

Dear Ruth—

Was I surprized when I got a letter from you!!

I havn't spoke to Lizzie Gould for a couple a years—she never comes to Relief Corps anymore & when she shows up to church she never stays after. I guess shes friendly enough, but she always acts like shes gotten something more important on her mind. I guess thats what the troubles all about.

The first I heard anything—our preacher's wife told some of us that Lizzie was threatening to leave Tom Gould. Probly last year sometime. Seems he needed her in the barn or something like that and when she woodent come he was forced to go in the house & drag her out. I can believe it. She always was such a stickler. In school she always had to be right. As you say I guess its the Humphrey in her. With all them babies, you would of thought she would think twice before making a fuss about a thing like that. They got at least seven or eight & the youngest cant be more than a couple weeks old. Well, it might of been a month since I heard at Relief Corps shes had another one.

That's about all I heard. Mr. Thurlow came home and said that the teacher up to the ridge was saying in the store the other day that the oldest Gould girl had to give up schooling and stay home and take care of her little sister. Of course everyone knows that their oldest boy has left home. I dont know, maybe hes 15, maybe more. I heard Lizzie just took the latest one with her, but from what you wrote I guess there must of been two.

Theres been a lot of talk. I guess most everyone blames her. He used to be ailing quite a lot, but from what they say he's doing pretty good right now. He got swamp fever or something during the War you know—pretty bad. But that dont give her no reason to skidoodle. If I'd of run off every time Mr. Thurlow had a ache, I would have gotten to China by now.

Well that's that. I hear the Lisbon GAR has invited units from all over Maine to come here to march on Decoration Day. If the Gray outfit comes, you plan to come to. It would be good to see you after all these years.

Best wishes
Rachel Thurlow

June 1, 1885

Dearest Mamma:

Father says he cannot understand why you do not come back and I do not know what to tell him, even if I think I know why. He says to tell you when I write to you that he thinks you are a good mother and he would be glad if you would be a good wife. That was what he said to tell you. Louise goes down to Aunt Aphia's every afternoon on her way home from school to see if there is a letter from you. When there is, I read it aloud to the children. Sometimes Grace has been very good about helping me about the house. Frank and Lillie are well. Lillie's new teeth are coming in. We miss you.

Your daughter Mary Emma

❧   ❧   ❧

Lizzie was uncertain when it was she first considered divorcing Tom. That Sunday morning as she left the farm she expected never to return, but the thought of a legal divorce did not occur to her. Divorce was not something that proper ladies contemplated. She knew that a man, who had discovered his wife with another man in flagrante delicto (as the newspapers delicately described the activity), could sue for divorce, and his action would be supported by the entire community, clergy and laity alike. But a wife could prudently take this step only when her husband had deserted her, and possibly not until after the desertion was of several years duration. Rank gossip would overtake even this woman should she show interest in a second man before her divorce decree became final. For a woman to sue for divorce for no other reason than the desire for freedom was out of the question.

When Lizzie arrived at her parent's home, she found her father (73) in poorer health than she had anticipated. She had known that age had forced him to retire from his cobbler's shop, but he had shielded all his children from learning the full extent of his illness. Furthermore, his financial condition was declining. To pay his medical bills he had had to mortgage the home he and his wife had occupied for thirty-six years, and now he was falling behind in the payments. Before involving her brothers and sisters in this desperate problem, Lizzie sought legal counsel.

Leaving the babies with her mother, she took the stage into Lewiston to see Emerson and Briggs, Attorneys at Law. Mr. C. V. Emerson listened to her tale and, when he learned she had left her husband, asked if she planned a divorce. She replied that a divorce would be extremely complicated and disagreeable.

"Not at all," Mr. Emerson assured her. "It's probably easier to get a divorce in the State of Maine than anywhere else in the world."

"You must be mocking me."

"I certainly am not." He smiled indulgently. "In such matters, Maine prefers to make things easy." He leaned back in his chair and placed the tips of his fingers together. He continued as if he were addressing a jury. "Maine was settled by men with independent minds, Mrs. Gould, like your grandfather and mine. Why did they come to the Maine wilderness? A question one may well ask." He smiled and paused as though he was sharing private information. "And the answer? Primarily to avoid oppression at the hands of the Pecksniffs of Boston."

"I suppose that's true," said Lizzie.

"Oh, you know Mr. Pecksniff?" he asked, peering disdainfully over his glasses. "A character in Dickens."

"I've read Martin Chuzzlewitz," Lizzie said. "I suppose some narrow-minded Bostonians could be compared to Mr. Pecksniff."

"Yes, yes, of course," said Mr. Emerson, clearly disappointed that his literary reference had not elicited a respectful display of incomprehension. After reflection he continued: "In 1820 whenMaine separated from Massachusetts and became a state, that same spirit of independence that brought the settlers here in the first place was incorporated into their laws—the divorce law, in particular."

"How interesting," she said.

As she rode back on the stage Lizzie mulled over lawyer Emerson's disclosure. By the time she had arrived in Gray she had decided to discuss the possibility of a divorce with her father.

She found Moses in bed, where lately he was forced to repair even after the slightest exertion. He raised his head from the pillow and smiled as she entered his bedroom on tiptoes. When she told him what she had learned from the lawyer, he thought long, tugging slowly at his beard.

"There'll be a deal of chatter…You can expect that," he said finally. "But…I imagine if you don't divorce Thomas, it won't be long before he'll be divorcing you…He's used to a woman keeping house for him. Now that you're not handy anymore he'll be looking for somebody else, or I miss my guess…Especially, with a house full of youngsters."

"Oh, but I intend to get the children…just as soon as I have a place for them."

"Tom'll never let you have them," Moses insisted with unexpected vigor. "Yes, Elizabeth, you'd better sue for divorce right away and ask for the children."

Panting, he lay back on the pillow and stared at the ceiling with bleared eyes. Then he raised his head again.

"Bring me that box from the cubby hole over there near the mantle, and my spectacles," he said. While Lizzie got up to get the items, he continued. "I thought all along it was just cultch in that box but it's letters your sister Sarah Jane wrote. I've been reading them," he smiled wanly, "Preparing, I guess, for the discussions I will soon be having with her. It won't be long now till we'll be together."

"Oh, Father...," Lizzie started to speak. He took the box and held up his hand to indicate that she should remain quiet.

"Right here on top," he said, perching his glasses on the end of his nose and taking the cover off the box. "I was reading it just this morning. I think you ought to hear what she has to say. She wrote this just a few months before she passed away."

Lizzie reached for the paper he picked up.

"No," he said, "I'll read it to you. It's dated July 26, 1866 and she wrote:" (He read in a scarcely audible tone, pausing between phrases for breath.)

"I wonder if I should be willing to be such a slave to work as those people all are. No, I feel that I shall not. I could not marry for such a destiny. It cannot be a duty. Yet all praise women who toil every moment and never spend an hour in self-cultivation. I will never be such a drudge, however. Very likely, I shall never marry at all. Certainly, not now nor very soon."

CHAPTER 30

"Every mother should remember that there are three foods, and only three, which contain in proper proportions, food for every part of the body. They are milk, eggs and whole wheat. Entire wheat makes the best bread for a growing child, but if he eats white flour bread, let him eat it with meat broth, eggs or milk.

*"Oats, rye or corn meal, either white or yellow, are excellent grains, when well cooked, and any of them makes good food, combined with milk. Oat-meal or corn-meal should be cooked in a double boiler not less than three hours." **Science of Feeding Babies etc.**: H. Elizabeth Gould. Rebson Co. NY. (1916) Page 121.*

Gray, Maine
May 12, 1885

Dear brother Caleb:

Do you have any idea how bleak life has become for our parents? For several days now I have been here at home in Gray and, I'm afraid, none too soon. Although I was aware that Father was not well I was unprepared for how much he has failed. He spends much of his time in bed. He eats little, and what he eats he has trouble keeping down. I believe he is in much greater pain than he admits. Although Mother is nowhere near as ill as Father, she is not well and certainly does not have the strength to care for him in his present state. When I first got here, I suggested that I write you and the rest of the family, but he persuaded me not to alarm any of you.

Then over last weekend I discovered that he is in danger of losing the home. There is a mortgage which is in arrears and he has been threatened by the bank with foreclosure. Yesterday I went into Lewiston to talk with Mr. Emerson at the Emerson and Briggs law firm, for I wanted to find all the legal ramifications before I wrote to you and our brothers. Father said that in the past you have had dealings with Mr. Emerson. He was very generous with his time and comforting in his advice. He agreed to get in touch with the bank and find out what can be done to forestall further adversity. He also pointed out that Father's property is extremely saleable, located as it is near a tavern and livery stable halfway on a post road linking two thriving cities.

Caleb, I know no other way to tell you except to come right out and say it. I have left Tom Gould. You are well aware of the difficulties I have had. The other morning when brother Howard happened to come by the farm, I was in desperate spirits. I had no other choice. I left dear, sweet Mary Emma to watch out for the older children and took Helen and baby Edgar with me. I stayed that night with Howard and Sarah and the next day took the stage back to Gray, where I found the conditions I have described above. I am uncertain what I shall do to support myself, but I have no intention of ever returning to the Ridge.

Lawyer Emerson believes that I should sue for divorce. Indeed, it was his suggestion. He insists that it will not be difficult and that Tom can be legally required to pay for the expense. Father agrees. He believes that I will have a better chance of keeping the children if I bring the suit and that sooner or later Tom will ask for a divorce if I do not. Dear, dear Father, he even has assured me that sister Jennie would support me in this decision. Please, Caleb, do not tell me I am doing the wrong thing. I am in dire straits.

I am also writing to Avery and Howard about the circumstances here at home. I'll wait until I hear from all of you before I write Eliza. Emma stopped by when she heard I was home and learned of the situation.

With all my love,
H. Elizabeth

Northridge, New Hampshire
May 15, 1885

Dear Hannah Elizabeth,

Your letter came as a great surprise. I surely did not realize that Father was facing difficulties such as you describe. His latest letter, not more than a month ago, was cheerful and filled with his usual good-nature. I shall come to Gray as soon as possible, but because of the commitments I must meet on the Sabbath it will not be before next week.

I am, of course, distressed to learn that you have left Gould, but I know full well it was not a decision reached by my beloved sister without a great deal of prayerful consideration. I shall not chide you. My own good wife suggests that under the difficult circumstances you find in Gray the care of two children is far too great a burden for you and that possibly you will agree that little Helen should return with me to Northridge, until such time as you are again established.

Think about it. Know, my dear sister, that you are always in our prayers. Will see you next week no later than Tuesday.

In haste,
Bro. Caleb

The following week both Caleb and Avery returned to Gray. Avery examined his father and conferred with the local doctor. They agreed that the old man had, at best, only a few months to live. Lizzie sent word to Emma that her brothers were at home. On Saturday Emma and her husband drove over for the day. Back at home Emma wrote to their youngest sister who was still living north of Bangor, over one hundred miles away:

Dear Eliza,

I am sure that by this time you have a letter from Lizzie about the grim prospects for papa. We went up yesterday and spent the day with him. Caleb was just leaving when we got there, but I had a long talk with Avery. He had spoken with Dr. Moulton and they agreed that papa is failing very fast. He is so pale and feeble. It is unlikely that he will be with us for much longer. Mother is bearing up better than I expected. As you know, she has not been well, either. I know that you will feel you should come home for a last visit but the family will understand if you choose not to. Lizzie is giving them good care. It would be a long, burdensome trip for you, particularly after your recent travel to Lisbon during Lizzie's time. We are all grateful to you. There's little that you can do even if you arrive in good season, and Avery said to tell you that by the time you have made arrangements to come, in all probability it will be too late. Lizzie seems very sound for the ordeal she has been through.

Thanks to your devoted care, I should guess. She still seems peaked, but the last time I visited her in Lisbon there was the look of a scared rabbit in her eyes. That's gone. I don't know whether she has written you about it yet, but you will soon hear whether I mention it or not. She is planning to divorce Tom Gould. She left him a few weeks ago. Howard stopped by the farm one morning when she was at the end of her rope and she just up and left with him. She took the two babies and left the rest of the children with Mary Emma, who certainly seems a responsible young woman. But I guess you know all this.

I'm sure things are going to work out for Lizzie. She deserves it after spending all those years with that man. Lawyer Emerson promises her that Gould will have to pay the fees and he hopes that after things get settled she will have all the children. Caleb took little Helen with him when he went back to New Hampshire. He was afraid she would cry after her mother, but she and her Uncle Caleb were "buddies" (as the young people are saying) right away. Sarah has made the offer that she and Howard will take Lillian (or one of the other children) when things get straightened around. I guess the family will see to it that the children don't suffer, but of course until after the divorce is final they will be staying with their father, and only Heaven knows what that means.

I'm sorry I don't have better news about our parents, but be assured that with Lizzie's care they are doing as well as possible. Tell your little ones that their Aunt Emma loves them.

Emma

Wednesday

Mamma,

We all stay well. Ralph came up the other night and stayed for supper. Father asked him why he didn't come home and live, but he said he guessed not and that anyways he was thinking about going up to Portland or Portsmouth or even to Boston and look for a job. Neither one got angry, the way they usually do. Father even shook hands with him when he left. Grace stays up to the Porters with her friend Alice almost every day after school. Mrs. Porter says she doesn't mind, because they are such good friends. I don't mind, because Louise is a big help around the house and she does a good job of keeping the two little ones out of mischief. Grace always comes home in time for supper. When Father needs help in the barn he usually calls for Grace. He says she is his big girl.

Father says to tell you that he is sorry to hear that Grandfather Foster is so very sick. We were all sorry when we heard about it.

We are always glad when there is a letter from you waiting at Aunt Aphia's. Louise stops by every day on the way home from school and if there is one she runs all the way home so we can read it together.

Mary Emma.

In reply to a letter from Lizzie asking that he start legal divorce proceedings immediately, Lawyer Emerson wrote:

June 3, 1885

Mrs. H. Elizabeth Gould,
Gray, Maine.
My dear Madam,

It is with regret that I must inform you that obtaining a divorce will not be so easy as your request implies. First we must establish the facts on which your petition will be based. Then the petition must be presented to the court for a hearing date to be assigned. The hearing date may be during the next term of court, but it also may be delayed for a number of reasons, which I shall not go into here. When the divorce is finally granted, it will probably be granted "nisi" which means it will not be final until after a period of time established by the court.

When you stated in your letter that you would be unable to come to my office in Lewiston because of the grave illness of your father, I feared that this might involve even further delay. Fortunately, later this month I shall be required by other business to spend a couple of days in Portland. I shall let you know the exact date. On my return trip I shall be able to stop over in Gray for a few hours, and obtain from you the specifications I shall need to prepare my brief. This accommodation will reduce your legal fees substantially.

Meanwhile, be so kind as to prepare a list of the charges you believe can be used in court: examples of unseemly language, improper demands, excessive parsimony, or abusive treatment of either yourself or the children. Try as near as possible to establish the dates and locations of the incidents, and the names of any witnesses. It is very important to be specific and accurate, for any indication of error or misstatement would be extremely harmful to your case. We shall discuss this in more detail when I am able to visit.

Kindly inform me immediately if such a visit to your home in Gray would be both feasible and proper.

With sincere regards,
C. V. Emerson, Esq.

CHAPTER 31

"…If a child loses its appetite, close attention must be given to the feeding. Try to tempt the appetite with something quite new. An excellent article to meet such a need is egg and lemon prepared in the following way: Divide the white and yolk of one egg. Put the yolk into a tumbler and stir into it two tea-spoonfuls of white sugar. Beat the white to a stiff froth, then mix it well into the yolk and sugar, and add to the whole the juice of a lemon. Beat until it is smooth again after adding the lemon." **Science of Feeding Babies etc.: H. Elizabeth Gould. Rebman Co. NY, (1916) Pg. 37**

Gray, Maine
June 1, 1885

My Dear Children—Every one of you.

I am happy to read in Mary Emma's letter that you have all been good children. Remember that Mary has many things to do and every time you fail to do what she tells you to, you are making things more difficult for her. It is fine that Grace has a close friend and I am proud that she is welcome in her friend's home, but it would be sinful for someone to allow friendship to interfere with one's duty. Make sure, Grace, that you come straight home from school to see whether Mary Emma needs you. Only then may you go play with your friend.

I hope the rhubarb patch on the south side of the barn has not been forgotten. I failed to mention it in my earlier letters. If you haven't been eating it, I am sure that by now it has grown very big but it is still usable. You know how to make sauce, Mary, and this time of year a bowl of rhubarb sauce is as good as any spring tonic for regulating a person's digestion. Let Louise or Franklin pull it for you. It will grow back. Do not let the little ones have more than a small portion of the sauce at one time, for too much will act as a physic and upset them.

I am now alone with Grampy and Grammy Foster. All of your Uncles were here for a few days and Aunt Emma came over. She said that if I need her she can run in on short notice. Grampy Foster is not very hale. Although he got up and put on his clothes this morning, he is able only to sit on the porch and read the Journal. Your grandmother rocked Edgar to sleep and now both are taking naps. Uncle Caleb took Helen to New Hampshire with him. We dressed her up in her pink bonnet with the white lace on it and she rode away with her uncle like a grown-up lady. I was very sad to see her go, but she didn't make any fuss. She just smiled at her uncle and waved goodbye to her mother. I shall miss my dear little Helen, as I miss all of you.

I was glad to hear that Ralph came up and had supper with you, which reminds me. I guess I had better stop now so I can write to Ralph. I have not written him in a while and I must get a letter off to him today.

Continue to be good children and know that your mother thinks of you always. All my love,

Mother

❦   ❦   ❦

June 1, 1885

Dear Son Ralph;

Mary Emma writes me that one evening you had supper at the farm with your sisters and brother. I was very pleased to hear that news. Do it often, dear, because they need you. Mary Emma said in her letter that you were talking of going down to Boston looking for work. I do not think you should—but not only because of the temptations you will face in the city. I know you are a young man who resists evil in all its forms. No, it's because I hope you will stay near your sisters so that you can help if they need to call on you.

I have already written you that I shall not be returning to the farm. I do not know what else you have been told but I am sure you have learned by now that I have been to Lawyer Emerson in Lewiston about a permanent legal separation. There will be some sort of a hearing as soon as it can be arranged. I expect that when that happens Mr. Emerson will want you to tell about your being discouraged from finishing school.

Nevertheless, dear, should you still decide to leave, I must give you a word or two of caution. Take your Bible with you. Read it regularly and abide by its teaching. There is no greater wisdom. Be careful in choosing your friends. It is easy for a young man to fall in with loose companions. There are many clever but unscrupulous persons who are eager to lure inexperienced youth away from uprightness. Make sure your friends are church going. Avoid those who use vulgar language, or play cards and indulge in other forms of gambling, or drink rum. They are not worthy of your friendship. I am confident that there is no need for your mother to urge you to shun unrefined and brazen women. My gallant son has too much respect for himself and his family to allow a scheming wanton to entrap him.

Whatever you decide to do, sweet son, you can be certain that your mother thinks about you always and prays regularly for your safety. Please write. I long to get a letter from you. I am enclosing a postage stamp. All my love,

Mother

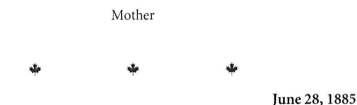

June 28, 1885

Dear Mary Emma,

Just a note to let you know that I shall be coming to Lisbon on July 4th with the Hodgdens, friends of Aunt Emma. Mr. Hodgden is marching in the parade. Aunt Emma will be staying here with Grandfather. I shall not be coming to the farm, but shall be visiting in the village with Mrs. Roberts. I think you know where she lives, but if you do not your Aunt Aphia can tell you. I want to see you and all the children. I am sure that all of you will be coming into town with your father to watch the celebration. You can slip into Mrs. Roberts' house after the parade goes by without his knowing anything about it. After I have held you all in my arms, then you can walk over to the park for the fireworks.

When I left I forgot to take the silk-lined box that I kept on the mantel in my bedroom. It holds a number of keepsakes I would like to have, if the box is still there. They belong to me and would have no value for someone else. Leave the box where it is and just wrap its contents in a handkerchief and carry them in your pocket. Then nobody will ask any questions. If the box has been moved by somebody or thrown away there is no need to ask anyone about it. The keepsakes have meaning only to me and I would not want you to get into any trouble. I shall be so happy to see my children.

> In haste
> Mother

❧   ❧   ❧

Mary Emma told none of the children that they were going to see their mother for fear the news might reach her father and he would forbid them even to go to the Fourth of July festivities. So not suspecting what was in store for them, they all, including their father, rode into the village in high spirits. Tom, with his beard trimmed and resplendent in his G.A.R. uniform, was in a playful mood, letting Louise and Franklin take turns holding the reins. Old Fan knew better than to let the childish tugs deflecther from the familiar route.

But after Tom had gone to join his comrades and as Mary Emma was finding a spot to watch the parade, Grace announced that her friends were waiting for her in front of the Post Office and she had no intention of staying with the family.

"We must keep together," Mary said firmly.

"You can't make me," declared Grace, stamping her foot.

"Well, after the parade goes by, we're all going over to Mrs. Roberts for a surprise."

"I don't like Mrs. Roberts."

"But, Grace."

"What kind of a surprise?"

"If I told you, it wouldn't be a surprise."

"Probably some of her old cookies. I'm not going." She started to walk toward the Post Office, swishing her skirts contemptuously. Mary ran after her and caught her by the arm.

"Mother's going to be there," Mary said, lowering her voice so that the smaller children could not hear.

Grace stopped.

"Mother!" she screamed. "What's she doing here?"

"Shh! She wants to see all of us."

"Well, I don't want to see her. Father said that Lawyer Moore told him to keep her away from us. Did you tell Father?"

"No, Father doesn't know."

"Well" Grace proclaimed defiantly and stalked off.

CHAPTER 32

"In too many families children of two years come to the table, eat anything they fancy or nothing. If the latter, they lunch, until the next meal, upon crackers or some sort of sweet food.

Contrast this picture with that of a low table neatly set, and each child comfortably seated. Plates are laid for all children under six years of age, and each is provided with fork, spoon and napkin. A mother is there, or some suitable caretaker, to teach correct table manners and to make the meal a happy one. **Science of Feeding Babies etc.**: *H. Elizabeth Gould. Rebman Co., NY. (1916) Pg. 124.*

It was nearly a year before the divorce action reached a hearing. By mid-August after several conferences with Lizzie, Lawyer Emerson finally had prepared a brief and was ready to submit it to the court. At the September term Tom, represented by Attorney Asa A. Moore, also filed a brief. The cases were continued from term to term, until on May 14, 1886 in the City of Auburn, County Seat for Androscoggin County, the two libels for divorce were tried together in S. J. Court, Judge J. Danforth presiding.

The Lewiston Evening Journal for that day reported the trial in explicit detail. The accusations were spelled out:

"Mrs. Gould charges in her libel for the last five years constant and gross neglect, ill treatment, abuse and great cruelty; that he has used to her obscene, profane and threatening language, called her vile and opprobrious names and treated her with great indignity, in May, 1883, an assault; that he compelled her to work upon the farm when quick with child, at the same time doing her own work in the house; that he has neglected to provide suitable food and clothing; that he is possessed of a quick, unreasonable and ungovernable temper; unfit to have the custody of children, has used profane and obscene language before them; that he has valuable real and personal property. She prays for a divorce; for dower in his real estate; reasonable alimony or instead thereof such sum as the court shall seem meet; and for the custody of each and all the children.

"Thomas J. Gould...charges his wife for four years past with extreme cruelty, cruel and abusive treatment, the use of abusive, reproachful, provoking, angry and wicked language; has expressed a desire to have his property wasted; endeavored to set the children against their father; attempted to pervert their youthful minds, endeavored to draw them into the practice of falsehood, deceit, treachery, dissimulation and other wickedness; has urged Ralph to abandon his father; encourages Mary in wicked and corrupt practices by carrying on with her a clandestine correspondence; that she possesses a perverse, obstinate, willful and spiteful disposition; that without any just cause, on the 20th of April 1885, she abandoned his home and six children and has continued such abandonment ever since; wherefore he prays right and justice and the custody of his children."

The Journal account went on to give the names and birth dates of the children and then a list of relatives of both libellants and their homes and occupations. After that the article continues with a discussion of the trial:

"Mrs. Gould's libel was first heard. She was the principal witness and is certainly a woman of intelligence and culture. She belongs to a brainy family; she comes from Gray and is connected with the Humphreys in that section, her maiden name was Foster; her mother was a sister *[In fact, Eliza Foster was a Benson, a cousin to the Humphreys. The newspaper account was incorrect.]* of Meshach Humphrey whom older politicians will remember as a Senator from Cumberland, an easy and eloquent speaker. Her father [is] Moses B. Foster...still living at Gray...a manufacturer of boots and shoes for more than forty years till compelled to stop by ill health..."

With Edgar snuggled against her shoulder, Lizzie arrived at the court house nearly an hour before her case was called, accompanied by her brother Dr. Avery Foster, whose practice was in Lewiston across the Androscoggin River, and Sarah, wife of Howard who was currently employed as a machinist at the Hill Mill, also in Lewiston. Attorney Emerson was awaiting them. He described his strategy. Because he had learned that Mr. Moore, Tom's attorney, was calling both Ralph and Grace to the stand as well as their father, he had decided that only Lizzie would have to testify on her behalf. "Through my cross-examination of the children, I'll beable to bolster our case," he declared.

When Avery learned that his testimony would not be required, he wished his sister well and departed immediately for his office. Sarah walked the corridor with the baby in her arms while Lizzie and Mr. Emerson conferred on a bench outside the court room. Edgar was sleeping soundly. Lizzie watched in dismay as the court filled with the curious, a number of whom she recognized as neighbors from both Lisbon and Gray.

As the newspaper article implied, Lizzie was a good witness, telling her story in a straightforward manner that appealed to the spectators in the court, as well as leaving, as far as anyone could tell, a favorable impression with Judge Danforth.

As for Tom and his testimony the reporter for the Journal had this to say:

"His appearance is peculiar, he was continually changing position; while testifying, sometimes sitting, sometimes standing and sometimes walking. He impresses you as conscientious, morbidly so, very nervous, thinks he always intends to do right, that he occasionally steps over the bounds of propriety. He is a member of the church, is almost as ready to confess his own faults as those of his wife."

"Sit down, if you please, Mr. Gould," Mr. Moore directed his pacing client after some preliminary questioning had brought Tom to his feet. Tom glanced across at the two fellow veterans who had come with him, now sitting on a bench against the west wall. They responded with a wink and a flicker of a nod. Tom sat.

"Now. tell us. Are you a profane man?"

"I don't believe so."

"Do you ever use profane or obscene language?"

"Not regular."

"Occasionally?"

"Only when I'm good an' provoked."

"Is that often?"

"I can think of only five times."

"Only five times?"

"Ayuh, that's all."

"Can you tell us when they were?"

"Ayuh. Once, when my wife's sister was nursin' her. I seen a lot o' dust on the mantel piece and I said it was a—" he paused and looked at the judge before he continued. The judge was impassive. "—a damned dirty hole."

Lizzie and Sarah exchanged glances and nodded in agreement.

"And other times?" his lawyer continued.

"One time when my wife an' my mother were quarrelin' and kickin' up a real fuss, I said to 'em I wished that damnation had 'em both." Nervously, Tom stood up again.

"That's twice, Mr. Gould."

"One time I remember, I was talkin' to my daughter Mary Emma. My wife had to put her tongue in and I turned to her and said, 'Damn your soul t' hell.'" Tom moved away from his chair and began to chuckle as he thought of what he was about to say. "Another time a bee stung me on the end o' my nose an' I said 'damn you'…meanin' the bee, of course. But I guess my wife heared me."

"That's four times."

"I don't know. There was another time, but it was her blame. She said somethin' raw, like she's always doin'. Look, I don't even curse at my oxen. Every farmer I know gets provoked with their oxen all the time but I never—never!—swear at mine."

"Those were the only times?"

"As far as I recollect."

When it came time for Mr. Emerson to cross-examine, he asked Tom:

"It has been testified that you use obscene language—sometimes in front of your children. Is that true?"

"It's hard to tell. Depends on what you mean by 'obscene'."

"Do you, yourself, think that you're sometimes obscene?"

"If you mean: Do I like a good story? I guess the answer is 'yes'." Tom looked across the courtroom toward his comrades who were smiling and nodding in agreement. They broke into laughter when he caught their eyes. Judge Danforth rapped for order. After a pause, calculated to call attention to the interruption, Mr. Emerson cleared his throat and asked:

"Have you ever used obscene language in front of your wife and children?"

"I guess I know what you're talkin' about," Tom replied sheepishly, as he moved back to the chair and sat down.

"Tell us about it,"

"Does she want me to repeat it?" For the first time during his testimony he glanced toward Lizzie and she looked away. He stood again.

"Tell us," directed Mr. Emerson.

"I called her a name. But I won't repeat it unless she says I have to."

Lawyer Moore called Ralph to the stand. Almost sixteen and overweight to the point of tubbiness, he was decked out in a new wool suit with a bright paisley vest and a string tie, his hair was barber-trimmed and his upper lip sported a downy, light brown moustache. As he rose he deposited his shiny derby on the seat.

Lizzie scanned him in amazement as he swaggered to the stand. She had not seen him enter the court room, or, if she had, she had not recognized him. Although this was the first time he had seen his mother in months, he had not gone over to speak to her. Lizzie was stunned.

Prompted at first by his father's attorney, Ralph was soon describing without assistance how his mother had encouraged him to leave home, how she had interfered with his father's discipline of the younger children, how disgusted he had been when he learned that she had abandoned her family.

Lawyer Emerson in cross-examination was able to get him to admit that it was possible his mother's motivation for encouraging him to leave home was so that he could finish his schooling, but he would not agree that his father was frequently unreasonable in his demands or that he used objectionable language.

Grace testified without ever looking at her mother. She corroborated her father's charge that there had been a clandestine correspondence between her mother and her older sister. She recounted how on the Fourth of July she had almost been tricked into seeing her mother when she didn't want to, in fact, had been ordered not to by her father. She said she thought there were other secret exchanges between Mary Emma and her mother, but this was challenged by Mr. Emerson and the judge ordered the statement stricken from the record.

CHAPTER 33

"Green Pea Soup—Large peas, a little too hard to be used as a vegetable, may be utilize in this soup.

INGREDIENTS
1 pint shelled peas
3 pints water
1 small onion
1 tablespoon butter or fat
1 tablespoon flour
Salt and pepper

"Put peas and onion in boiling water, and cook from 1/2 to 1 hour, till very soft. Press through colander.

"Add to the above, 1 pint stewed tomatoes and a little more seasoning. This is excellent, combining the nutrition of the pea and the flavor of the tomato." **Science of Feeding Babies etc.:** *H. Elizabeth Gould. Rebman Co., NY. (1916) Pg. 128*

"And now all and singular in the premises being seen, heard and fully understood and the material facts alleged in the libel duly proved to the satisfaction of the Court, on the twenty-third day of the term being the fifteenth day of May, A.D. 1886, it is ordered and decreed by the Court in favor of said Hannah Elizabeth Gould that the bonds of matrimony existing between her and the said Thomas J. Gould be dissolved NISI for the cause of cruel and abusive treatment.

"It is further ordered that said libellant have the care and custody of the minor children Mary E. Gould, Louise H. Gould, Helen S. Gould and Edgar W. Gould during said six months and until the further order of the Court & that she recover of the libellee the sum of eight hundred dollars in lieu of alimony and dower.

"This decree is to become absolute after the expiration of six months from the fifteenth day of May A.D. 1886 upon compliance with the terms hereof or on application of either party to the Clerk of Court, unless the Court has for sufficient cause, on application of any party, otherwise ordered."

So concludes the record of the Androscoggin County Clerk of Courts in the divorce proceedings of T. J. and H. E. Gould.

❧   ❧   ❧

Lizzie was free, but freedom brought formidable obligations. For months she had been living hand-to-mouth. Now, she needed an immediate infusion of money. But Tom insisted through his attorney that it would be impossible for him to come up with so great an amount of cash before the middle of summer, and even then the full sum of $800 would be unlikely. He was permitted to sign a note, putting his farm up for security, agreeing to pay in full by the first of September.

Although it was true that Mary Emma had become available to her mother to help with the care of her grandparents, it was equally a fact that her addition to the household, as well as Sister Louise, put an extra strain on Lizzie's already limited resources. Moses' remaining days were probably few, but plans for the future had to include Lizzie's mother who was still "getting around" and requiring a great deal of care.

When she had first notified her brothers of the serious state of their father's finances, they had responded, providing money to stabilize his mortgage temporarily. But now she found her brothers and sisters, with their own problems and families, were only too willing to turn the responsibility for the parents over to the sister who was "living at home". Avery suggested a number of doctors of his acquaintance who might find employment for Mary Emma as a companion for well-to-do, elderly patients. Also, for Lizzie's possible use, he provided names of families who could benefit from her experience in child care.

Lizzie knew nothing of finance. Before her marriage her father had handled her money and for the past seventeen years she had seen hardly enough cash to be able now to identify different units of currency. Suddenly thrust into circumstances requiring a knowledge of budgeting, mortgages, and deeds, she found herself face to face with an obscure mystery.

At the Lewiston bank that held the mortgage on her father's home the middle-aged son of the founder led her into a dismal office reeking with tobacco smoke. On the expanse of his ample vest she noticed several holes burned by hot cigar ashes.

"Mrs. Gould," he suggested avuncularly as soon as she had explained her errand, "Perhaps it would be more expeditious if this matter were discussed with Mr. Gould."

"This is not Mr. Gould's concern," she explained. "The property belongs to my father, who is too ill to handle it himself."

"Aye, yes. Then a brother, perhaps. Do I understand that you have brothers, Mrs. Gould?"

"Several. But I am the one who is living at home."

"Well, Mrs. Gould." He paused as though exploring other male possibilities beside the three already mentioned. When he could think of none he continued:

"Very well, Mrs. Gould. However, I would recommend that you discuss the matter with your husband. I am sure that he can advise you as well as I can on a matter so elementary as the payment of debts."

"My husband and I have separated."

"What?"

"Yes. We are divorced."

"Madame?" he intoned, more as if it were a question than a means of address. He straightened in his chair as he spoke and glanced across her shoulder to the door he had closed when they had entered the office. He reached for the corner of his desk and pulled himself erect. "Aye, yes, don't you find it a bit close in here." He crossed and opened wide the door, nodding brusquely to the teller behind the grille as if to make certain that his action had been observed. "Now, let's see, Mrs. Gould," he went on in a much louder voice, "It was the mortgage on the Foster home, your father's, we were discussing."

Lizzie's annoyance at the implications of his behavior became apparent at once. Her face reddened. She started to speak, but the rush of words jammed in her throat. Tears welled up. She rose and started to leave, but had to turn back to pick up the purse and gloves she had placed on the table. Her shoulders shook. The banker watched without any apparent comprehension.

"I was asking only for information," she murmured, as she swished her skirts through the door, across the lobby and out to the street.

❀   ❀   ❀

She returned to Gray irritated and disappointed. As she descended from the stage in front of the Midway Inn, Harry Foote, the owner, removing his hat, came down the steps to greet her.

"You're Lizzie Foster, ain't you? Moses' daughter?"

She was not ready for his friendly smile. Still rankled by the banker, she imagined disapproval lurking behind (what seemed to her) Foote's mocking smirk.

"I'm now Mrs. Gould," she snapped.

"I thought I recollect you. Went up to the house this mornin' to talk to your father but the young lady there said he wa'n't well enough to see anybody."

She gasped. In her resentment of the banker she had assumed that all society condemned her. Now, she had almost rejected someone who was trying only to be congenial. She resolved not to make such a mistake again.

"He's very sick," she murmured after the moment it took for her to regain her composure.

"P'raps you can tell me. Do you think he'd sell that back parcel of his lot? Maybe quarter of an acre, maybe more. I see he hain't put a garden in for a couple years."

"You want to buy some of my father's land?"

"Maybe. Since the railroad's gone through, folks ain't comin' up the pike like they used to. I got a couple notions, but I'll need more land and if Moses don't be askin' too much, I might be persuaded to talk to 'im...."

❀   ❀   ❀

Lizzie decided not to tell her brothers and sisters of Foote's offer until after she had Lawyer Emerson's advice. In a six page letter to him she wrote in detail the possibilities she saw for the future: By selling a small portion of the land, the mortgage could be cleared; then she would be free to stay in her parents' home as long as her father lived; (would Lawyer Emerson explain how mortgages were foreclosed?); meanwhile, on the strength of her brother's recommendation she had been able to find several temporary positions as a practical nurse (mostly with sickly children) where her knowledge of nutrition was most valuable; the pay was not much but kept food on the table; while she was away Mary Emma was seeing to her grandparents and the younger children; as soon as possible she hoped to rent smaller quarters and sell the big house, which needed much repair; etc.; etc.

She received his reply dated July 10:

Dear Madame:

I received this forenoon a line from Thos. J. Gould in which he asked that we be at home Monday between 4 and 5 p.m. and he would call and "make some arrangement about taking it up" his exact words are enclosed in quotation marks. I don't understand if or not he is to pay the money on that day or it will not be done for a few days later than that. But I want you to sign the enclosed paper and forward to me by the earliest mail so that I may be prepared to cancel the mortgage if he comes prepared to pay the am't due and that will avoid the necessity of your coming up or at any rate until I get the money for you.

Regarding the mortgage on your father's place…*(There follow several paragraphs answering her questions on mortgages. Then he concludes.)*

I was glad to hear from you and hear of your prosperity and the continued good health of you and the children and so far as tiring of the details you wrote about—I shall ever be glad to hear them and if I can help you be too glad to do so.

I think Mrs Gould that you have done wisely…it looked to me as I was there that your fathers building would soon require extensive repairs—but more than that you have a great load on your shoulders and I think all one woman should undertake. I think you have done for the best.

I hope this may reach you Monday in season for you to return the enclosed Monday afternoon. Sign your full name please Hannah Elizabeth G_____.

Truly yours
C. V. Emerson

🍁   🍁   🍁

The meeting between Emerson and Tom went off as scheduled on Monday afternoon, but the signed paper from Lizzie did not arrive at the lawyer's office until Tuesday morning. Since Tom was prepared to pay the $800 in full, this created only a slight delay before the money was in Lizzie's hands.

A few weeks later, Mary Emma received a letter from her father saying her grandmother had died. Lizzie made arrangements for the two older girls to attend Rebecca's funeral. The old lady was laid to rest, not in the Gould family lot high above the Androsoggin where Jacob, her husband and Tom's father, was buried with his first wife, but in a small plot in the cemetery on the Ridge purchased almost forty years before when her daughter Mary had died in infancy.

Moses died in the autumn and only a few days later, when Louise went to her grandmother's bedroom to bring the old lady her breakfast, she found that she had died peacefully during the night.

🍁   🍁   🍁

From: Emerson & Briggs, Attorneys at Law
Lewiston, Maine
To: Mrs. H. Lizzie Gould
     Gray, Maine
     January 11, 1887

Dear Madame—

I received your kind letter some time since—and neglect is partly an excuse for so long a delay in answering.

I was glad to hear that you and your family are doing so nicely—and I know that you must be enjoying yourselves better than in the years gone by—at least some of them. I do think your prospects are encouraging and cheerful—I was glad to hear of Mary's change of idea—viz.: education. I hope she may not be hindered in now rapidly advancing in her different studies.

I sympathize with you Mrs. Gould in your recent affliction. It was not wholly unexpected and yet it is hard indeed to endure the loss of those near and dear to us as Father and Mother. I do hope you may find such consolation as is possible in so great bereavement.

I was glad to meet recently your brother Caleb and wish the interview could have been longer.

Now for a little business—your divorce was granted as you recollect "nisi" meaning conditional—and to be made absolute after 6 months by proper petitions etc. etc. Six mos. have elapsed & Mr. T. J. Gould sent me word that he wanted me to take out the final papers. Petition for final papers may be made by either party and the final order is the same precisely as if you had made the petition.

I have not yet answered him—wishing to first hear from you and this is the only difference I know of—I have stood by you and shall—I know you have believed in me and I do not now propose to shake your confidence in me in the least. If I act for you in this matter I shall charge you nothing. If I act for him I shall charge him the regular fee and I would like to hear from you as soon as convenient in the matter.

In neither case will you be required to be present as the decree is formal and testimony is rarely needed or used.

I apprehend Mr. G. wants this done that the 2 yrs. limit which must expire before he can remarry, may begin to run as soon as possible. Of course I only suspect in this latter tho't.

I want you to feel and rest assured that I am firmly wedded to your interests and to your side of the cause in all of this domestic trouble—I don't know as I have explained myself clearly or my position understandably—if not I would be glad to further shed any light possible.

And now hoping you finely and the little ones too—I will close by saying—shall always be glad to hear from you and in the future will try to be more prompt in answering—I am

Most truly yours
C. V. Emerson.

CHAPTER 34

"New England baked beans are well suited to the needs of growing children, but some methods of baking them fail to bring out their full value.

"There is nothing about a bean which needs to be gotten rid of; therefore, to parboil and pour off the water must be a mistake.

"Measure and wash in two waters two cupfuls of pea-beans or yellow-eyes. To each cupful allow two tablespoons of olive oil and one small teaspoon salt. Soak overnight in four cups (one quart) cold water, but do not drain.

"In the morning pour beans, and water, if any, into an earthen bean pot with close cover, which should be one-half to two-thirds full. The remaining space is to be filled with boiling water.

"Beans should be baked five hours with steady heat. Keep the pot well filled with water for the first three hours, but toward the last lower the heat a little, letting them boil down slowly. **Science of Feeding Children etc.:** H. Elizabeth Gould. Rebman Co., NY. (1916) Pg. 131.

Although Lawyer Emerson continued to handle both sides of the divorce case during the six months before the separation became absolute, there is no evidence that this conflict of interest seemed important to Lizzie.

Toward the end of January, she received this letter from their mutual attorney:

Dear Madame:—

Mr. T. J. Gould desires that I say to you that if you will go back to Lisbon and take back some things you have said—be a humble and good wife—do your part towards making a happy home etc. etc., he will be glad to have you do so.

I have written this to please him and I know it will amuse you and, too, it may provoke as well, but I feel it is so typical of the man that you will be amused.

I have his application signed for final decree etc. etc. but wait to hear from you before filing it with the court.

I know now, Mrs. Gould, just what your answer will be but, to satisfy his importunity, want it from your own pen.

Can you answer so I will get it tomorrow?

I enjoyed your last very much—they are never too long for me to carefully read.

In haste and as ever—very truly,

C.V.E.

The following excerpt is a further and final citation from the records of the Androscoggin County Clerk of Court concerning the divorce:

"...On the tenth day of February A.D. 1887...Thomas J. Gould filed his application for a final decree.

"And now on the tenth day of February A.D. 1887 being after the expiration of six months from the entry of the degree NISI application having been made by the said Thomas J. Gould to the Clerk of said Court to have said decree NISI made absolute and a final decree entered herein and the Court not having otherwise ordered the said decree is made absolute and final."

Lizzie wrote to Emerson to ask about the four children the court had awarded to Tom. Now that the divorce decree was final, would it be possible, for her to assume custody of all of them? He replied that when he had asked Tom about the children, "Mr Gould told me Ralph was away from home but nothing more than that." Lizzie already knew this.

A few days later the Lisbon friends, whom Grace had been staying with (one might even say, "clinging to", for she seldom was at the farm), brought her to Gray and with little ceremony turned her over to her mother. They insisted that she was "so dreadfully homesick for her family." However, after a discussion with Grace, Mary Emma confided to her mother that her younger sister had confessed she had refused to return to the farm only because her father made her work too hard. The neighbors, she had admitted, no longer wanted the responsibility for her care.

This left only eight-year-old Franklin and Lillian, two years younger, at the farm with their father. Although Emerson had not indicated that Lizzie had any legal right to the children awarded to their father, she could not avoid observing that Tom had raised no objection when Grace departed. She decided that he would probably say nothing if the care of little Lillian were also transferred to her mother. A bleak farm with no women in the household was hardly a place to bring up a little girl.

In his memoir "A Maine Man in the Making" (Franklin F. Gould, Harper and Bros. Publishers, NY. (1950) Pg. 4ff) Franklin describes the day his older sisters came to get Lillian:

"Inside the schoolhouse, an overgrown girl was trying to teach subjects with which she was unfamiliar to twenty pupils who ranged in age from four years to a mustached boy in the back seat. All twenty were fidgeting in their seats and watching the clock as if hypnotized. The hands of the clock appeared to be stationary but they were slowly moving toward the four o'clock that would send the children whooping down to their homes.

"I was the tousled-headed boy in the next-to-the-back seat, and I had my doubts as to what four o'clock would bring. I had seen my big sisters whispering to the teacher while they looked at me in a furtive manner that boded me no good. My little sister sat in the seat ahead of me but she couldn't tell me for which one of my crimes I was about to be punished, so I fidgeted with the others but not for the same reason.

"The blow fell when school was dismissed. 'Frank. you will remain and study your geography for one hour.' My spelling could have stood another hour's study but my geography was good, so I knew there was something afoot they didn't want me to know. The big sisters dragged the little sister with them when they went, and I was fearful of what they would do to her when I was not around with my cowhide boots to take her part....

"When my hour was up, I shot out of the schoolhouse like a bullet from a gun and raced down the road with my feet slapping the road dust into a cloud that stretched back to the schoolhouse. As I turned into the dooryard I was calling: 'Lillie, Lillie,' at the top of my voice, but there was no answer except the hungry bawl of the bull tied in the barn. I raced through the house calling Lillie's name, but only found bureau drawers dumped on the floor and the sink full of dirty dishes. I rushed down to the barn hoping the girls were doing the chores, but my cries echoed back from the empty lofts. I found the old mare missing from her stall and the democrat wagon from the carriage house. I ran to the nearest neighbor and learned that they had been seen driving down the road. Back at the house I lighted a lamp and found a paper lying on the cold stove. 'We have gone to Mother's and taken Lillie with us,' it said.

"Father had gone to Lewiston with a load of produce. He had been gone all day and would be home soon but I needed him too badly to wait. I started up the road running as fast as I could; when I was out of breath I would throw myself down and cry until I could run again. Miles out on the road Father found me beside the road sobbing: Father, they have run away and taken Lillian with them.'

"He made no sound as he lay me on the wide seat and put my head in his lap. Then he took off his coat and covered me from the night's chill and, stroking my hair gently, he spoke to the horses. The harness squeaked and the old market wagon wobbled and rattled as the horses got in motion to carry Father and me home to an empty house."

It is not recorded how Old Fan and the democrat wagon were returned to the farm, but it would be no less than a historical fact to report that Tom did not rest until they were back in his barn.

Epilogue

Nineteen-sixteen, the year I was born, saw the publication of Grammy's book ("Science of FEEDING BABIES and Normal Care of the Growing Child for Nursing Mothers and Infants' Nurses"). Without any formal training as a nurse she had established a reputation throughout much of New England as a nutritionist, particularly in regard to the care of children recovering from diphtheria, a scourge rampant across the world in the early years of the last century. The book was not a financial success, but because it offered practical suggestions for a young mother it had many enthusiastic advocates.

My own memories of Grammy are meager. For at least a couple of years before her death in 1927 she was bedridden. She was living with Aunt Lillian about sixty miles from where I grew up, so I saw her rarely and each time for only a few minutes. Before that I remember her as a tiny woman with a round face and a constant smile. It has been said that I resemble her, which may account for my recollection that she was especially fond of me. Otherwise, I recall that when asleep she snored loud and vibrantly.

Her life certainly became no easier after the divorce. In her correspondence with her children she constantly refers to her lack of money, frequently explaining her delay in answering a letter because she couldn't afford postage. But her life was no longer cramped. She was free from the isolation of the farm wife. She was meeting interesting people and she became involved in the causes that especially appealed to her such as universal suffrage and the temperance movement.

Over and over she faced tragedy. In November, 1902, the dreaded "white plague" (tuberculosis) took my Aunt Louise. Grammy wrote heartbreaking letters to her other children as she nursed Louise through the final months of illness. Even before Louise's death the family learned from Grammy that her youngest daughter, Helen, had also contracted the disease. Aunt Helen died in 1904 just as the New Year came in. Later both Aunt Lillian and Uncle Eddie came down with TB. He died in 1913. After months in the sanatorium at Saranac Lake, New York, Aunt Lillian was sent home to Maine as incurable. She found a job teaching in a rural school, requiring her to walk several miles a day to and from her residence. (How little was known at that time about the transmission of disease and the care of the sick!) Miraculously, despite this regimen she recovered her health and lived into her eighties. Both Aunt Mary and Uncle Ralph lost their spouses to the same pestilence.

In spite of their spotty upbringing, the children of Tom and Lizzie gave, on the whole, a good accounting of themselves.

Uncle Ralph became a successful country storekeeper in Harmony (and later Anson), Maine, where he established some distinction as a Yankee story teller. After retiring he wrote several autobiographical best-sellers and for a time was a popular guest on Boston radio talk shows.

When Aunt Mary's husband, Charles Moody, died in Colorado, where they had moved with their five children after being advised that the high altitude might cure his tubercular cough, my father, Franklin, scraped together the money (with some help from his brother and sisters) to bring her and her family back east. She eventually became a teacher in the lower grades of the schools of Medford, Massachusetts. When the state legislature enacted laws requiring teacher training she had never obtained, the superintendent convinced Boston University to give her an honorary degree. Thus he was able legally to keep his best teacher.

Aunt Grace married Bert Moore who, during my childhood, ran a prosperous paint and hardware business in Springvale, Maine. The summer after Uncle Bert's death Dad sent me, still a teenager, to help Aunt Grace with the heavy lifting as she continued to run the store all by herself.

Dad became a Railway Postal Clerk, sorting the U. S. Mail between Boston and Bangor. After his retirement he wrote his own book, "A Maine Man in the Making", in which he recounted his life growing up alone with his father. This book also made *The New York Times* best seller list.

Aunt Lillian remained single. After recovering from TB, she studied bookkeeping and stenography. She was for many years the Assistant Clerk of Courts in the York County Court House in Alfred, Maine, serving under both Republican and Democratic Clerks as the political winds changed. There in the library one can find volumes of legal history recorded in her precise handwriting. Or later in her equally precise typing.

Neither Tom nor Lizzie remarried. Throughout the early years after the divorce each of their children visited with their father on the farm for various lengths of time until the big house was destroyed by fire in 1913, but the couple never saw each other again until shortly before Grammy's death when Dad prevailed on his father to visit his former wife. Aunt Lillian was not sure Grammy would recognize Grampy for the old lady's memory had been failing, but Grammy smiled wanly when the grizzled old man entered her bedroom. She said "Hello, Tom." Dad left them alone for the half hour they were together. There is no record of what they talked about.

When she died a few weeks later, Dad made arrangements for Grampy to be brought to her funeral. For me, an eleven-year-old watching from the side-lines, it was hard to tell whether Grampy was actually weeping or was just a bleary-eyed old man. He died a little over a year later.

The end

0-595-34286-8